SNOW JOB

Joe looked beyond the helicopter pilot at the snow blowing off the peak. "Fly into that plume of snow and go down low," he ordered the pilot. "We're going to jump out."

"Are you nuts?" Frank yelled. Just then the man in the other copter brought his Uzi up and snapped off a couple of shots into the air.

"If we jump out with our snowboards on," Joe said, "we can be moving as soon as we hit the ground."

"That just might work!" Frank exclaimed. "And if we hug the tree line on our way down the mountain, he won't have a clear shot at us."

As the helicopter took a steep dive, Joe put his boots into his snowboard bindings, then opened the copter door. He felt a blast of icy wind tearing at him as he hung his legs out. He paused only long enough to fit his goggles over his eyes.

"Geronimo!" Joe shouted. Then he leaped into the whiteness.

Books in THE HARDY BOYS CASEFILES® Series

Available from ARCHWAY Paperbacks

HEIGHT OF DANGER

FRANKLIN W. DIXON

AN ARCHWAY PAPERBACK
Published by POCKET BOOKS
New York   London   Toronto   Sydney   Tokyo   Singapore

AN ARCHWAY PAPERBACK *Original*

An Archway Paperback published by
POCKET BOOKS, a division of Simon & Schuster Inc.
1230 Avenue of the Americas, New York, NY 10020

Copyright © 1991 by Simon & Schuster Inc.
Produced by Mega-Books of New York, Inc.

ISBN: 0-671-73092-4

First Archway Paperback printing October 1991

10 9 8 7 6 5 4 3 2

Cover art by Brian Kotzky

Printed in the U.S.A.

IL 6+

HEIGHT OF DANGER

Chapter

1

"LOOK OUT BELOW!" Joe Hardy barreled down the steep slope on a sleek orange and blue snowboard. He stood sideways on the five-foot-long fiberglass plank, his feet tucked securely inside flexible, hard-soled nylon boots that were strapped into position by the board's bindings.

Ten yards behind him his eighteen-year-old brother, Frank, followed on a red snowboard. "Joe, cool it! You're going to mow somebody down!"

Frank, who was a year older than Joe, shook his head as he watched his brother hotdog down the mountain so fast he was just a bright blur against the snow in his blue racing suit with matching gloves and elbow and kneepads.

Joe ignored his brother's warning and continued to whiz along, using his arms to keep his balance. Several times he narrowly avoided running into the skiers who veered into his path. The cold mountain air bit into his face, and he was thankful that his goggles and helmet helped to cut the wind.

As he flew down the slope, Joe looked out over the majestic panorama of the Austrian Alps. He kept strong pressure on the front of his board and used his back foot to kick the tail around in a sweeping move that sprayed the powdery snow out behind him. He began to feel a rhythm to his ride, timing his curves smoothly with no pause in between.

Joe felt exhilarated as he began to master his snowboarding, as if he could take off and fly. Bending his knees, he carved a sharp, flashy right turn, only to find himself on a collision course with another snowboarder just ahead of him.

"Watch it!" Joe yelled, but the boarder didn't seem to hear him. In the instant before their boards collided, Joe threw his weight sideways from the knees and hips and carved a sharp turn back to the left—right into Frank's path.

"Joe—hit the snow!" he heard his brother shout.

With the reflexes of a born athlete, Joe Hardy threw all of the weight of his muscular six-foot frame to the right side of the snowboard. He saw Frank frantically swinging his arms in an effort to avoid him, but it was too late. The brothers collided in a tangle of arms and legs and boards, sliding several yards down the slope before they came to a stop. They both lay on their backs for a moment, laughing at themselves. The family resemblance was evident in their smiling features, but Joe was blue-eyed and blond and Frank had dark hair and eyes and stood an inch taller than his brother.

"Hey, guys, are you okay?"

Joe looked up and saw the snowboarder he'd nearly hit. He wore a dark blue nylon ski suit, which hung loosely on his skinny frame. His long blond hair was kept out of his face by a white headband and he spoke with a German accent.

"Let me give you a hand."

"Thanks!" Joe replied gratefully. He had found that the boards, which lacked the quick release bindings of skis, made it difficult to stand up after a spill.

"My name is Hans," the boarder said, pulling Joe up. "I work here at the resort, running one of the gondolas."

Joe brushed snow off his ski pants. Then he turned around and helped Frank to his feet. "I'm Joe Hardy and this is my brother, Frank," Joe said, extending his hand to Hans as skiers whooshed past them down the mountainside. "We're working security for the World Snowboarding Championships tomorrow."

"I saw you guys on some earlier runs," Hans

said with a friendly smile. "Your form's not bad. You're not beginners on these shred sleds."

"Joe won an amateur competition back home in the States," Frank said proudly. "That's how we got here. The prize was a trip for two to Graz, plus a chance to work behind the scenes at the championships."

"Great," Hans said enthusiastically. "Look me up at the lodge later, and I'll introduce you to the rest of the gang here. Boarders from all over Europe come here to work out during snow season."

Before Joe could respond, another boarder zoomed up beside them and slowed to a stop. The board was a star-spangled red, white, and blue, and its rider wore a matching ski suit.

Talk about good form, Joe thought with a mild twinge of envy. The grinning newcomer had practically stopped on a dime.

"Hi, Hans," the stranger said, pushing his dark hair out of his eyes. "How's it going?"

The boarder spoke with an American accent and eyed the brothers in a friendly, inquisitive way. He must be about twenty-five years old, Joe decided. But why did he look so familiar?

"I'm Frank Hardy and this is my brother, Joe," Frank said as he shook hands with the boarder.

"Nice to meet some fellow shredders." The tall stranger pushed his gray-lensed ski goggles up on his forehead, revealing his green eyes. "My name's—"

4

But before he could identify himself, Joe interrupted. "Ken Gibson, the American snowboarding champ. Wow! I didn't recognize you behind the goggles."

"That's me." Gibson looked amused. "I saw you guys fall into that pileup. I've knocked off practicing for the day. Can I offer you some tips?"

"That'd be great," Joe replied eagerly.

"Well, I see you're in good hands." Hans slipped his goggles back into place. "I go on duty at gondola number three in a few minutes. You guys should stop in at the employee lounge tonight. A lot of boarders and skiers hang out there."

"That kid's going to be a real competitor someday," Ken said as he watched Hans zoom down the slope, carving some graceful turns. "Are you two here to watch the snowboarding championships?"

"Actually, Frank and I are working security," Joe replied.

"Well, welcome aboard, guys. Ready for your first lesson?" Gibson looked downslope, trying to locate a clear area.

"Down there looks good," Gibson announced. He pointed to a spot about one hundred yards downhill. "Follow me."

Gibson shifted his weight onto his back foot and pivoted the front of the board around. Joe watched him lean forward and gracefully take off downhill, moving swiftly through a serpen-

5

tine series of left and right turns that took him exactly to the spot he had pointed out.

"Yahoo!" With an excited shout Frank took off after the American champion. He stayed on a straight course, holding his arms out from his sides as he tried to maintain his course and balance.

As Joe leaned forward to follow them, he tried to imitate the relaxed, easy way Gibson balanced into the turns. Already he felt more in control as he whizzed past the skiers and leaned low over the side of his board, dragging one hand in the snow to carve a turn that brought him right up to Gibson and Frank. Gibson nodded approvingly as Joe kicked up a roostertail of white powder before coming to a stop.

Joe swept his gaze over the snow-covered caps of the Austrian Alps. They were now halfway down the slope, a little to the side of the lifts and main trails. Below he could see the resort lodge with its large, glassed-in restaurant. Nearby, crowds of skiers and a few snowboarders milled around the loading area for the gondolas and chair lifts. Farther down the mountain he could just make out the tiny Austrian village of Graz, with its picturesque houses and inns.

"Not bad," Gibson commented, patting Joe on the shoulder. "Once you learn how to control your turns a little better, I think you'll have it knocked."

"How about me?" Frank asked eagerly.

"You're keeping your board too flat when you

turn," Gibson explained. "You need to alter your center of gravity and work on shifting your balance from side to side. That helps the edges of the board bite into the snow and keeps you from skidding."

"When I try to refine my turns, I lean over too far and fall on my side," Joe said.

Gibson shrugged with a good-natured smile. "It took me a lot of hours before I felt in control on my downhill runs."

Gibson's advice was cut off by a hissing sound upslope. Joe looked around just in time to see a short, stocky snowboarder with sandy crew-cut hair zoom down to them, stopping in an enormous swirl of powder. His red safety helmet matched his jacket and the stripe on his black ski pants. The small flag patched on his shoulder marked him as an American, and Joe judged him to be no older than twenty.

"I hope you guys aren't paying for lessons from this windbag," he said, pushing his goggles up off his face. "If you are, you'd better get your money back now. By this time tomorrow he'll be flying home with the rest of the losers."

"What rock did you crawl out from under, Warburton?" Gibson said in a bored, impatient voice.

"What's the matter, Gibson?" Buck Warburton prodded, a defiant expression settling on his wide face. "Can't stand hearing the truth about yourself?"

"You're so full of hot air, Buck," Gibson said

blandly. "What are you trying to prove, that you're some big hotshot on the slopes?"

"I can sure beat you, buster. On the slopes or off!"

He made a move toward Gibson, but Joe reached out to stop him. "Hey, why don't you settle down?" Joe suggested calmly.

Warburton glared at Joe. "Settle down, huh? Says who?"

"Joe Hardy. This is my brother, Frank. We're working security for the competition," Joe snapped.

"Oh, wow. I feel more secure already," Warburton said sarcastically. "You poor boys ought to pick your friends better," he added as he prepared to zoom off again toward the ski lifts. "You take lessons from amateurs, you might pick up some bad habits."

Warburton pushed off downhill, calling back to Ken Gibson, "Break a leg, Gibson. I mean that!" Then he disappeared in a swirl of powder.

As Joe stared after him, outraged, Frank turned to Ken Gibson. "Who was that creep?" he asked.

"Another contender for the championship," Gibson replied dryly. "Buck's not a bad snowboarder, but he's a lousy sport. I slaughtered him in the American competition, and he can't stand the idea that someone might be better than he is."

"But he acts like he really hates your guts," Joe observed.

Smiling, Gibson shook his head before replying, "He's just mad because he can't get me to lose my cool. I've beaten Buck plenty of times, and I'll beat him tomorrow, too."

"Look, there goes Mr. Personality right now," Joe said, pointing to the nearest chair lift. Warburton rode in one of the chairs just starting up the slope. "I can't wait to see what moves he comes up with this time," he added sarcastically.

"Forget Buck," Ken said. "What were we talking about?"

"Turning technique," Frank reminded him.

"Oh, yeah. Now watch me." Gibson pivoted on the heel of his board so that he faced Frank and Joe.

"Turns are accomplished mostly with upper-body movements. They don't have to be big—no arm waving and stuff." He grinned at Frank, then demonstrated the movements while standing still. "See, it's just a slight bending of the torso. You balance yourself with your arms."

Joe watched, then tried to copy Ken's movements. The next time he looked up, he noticed that the athlete had stopped cold and seemed to be listening to something up the slope.

"What's that?" Ken asked in a low voice.

"What's what?" Joe, too, stopped to listen. He glanced at Frank, who shrugged.

Then Joe heard it. A low, distant rumbling, like an avalanche. Joe looked around wildly, but then he realized that he didn't feel any vibration in the slopes beneath his feet.

"I don't see anyth—" he started to say as he turned back to Ken. But one look at Ken's face stopped the words in his throat.

Ken stared over Frank's shoulder at something up the mountain. Suddenly he snapped into action. "Watch out!" he screamed, too stunned to move.

Joe whirled around. Directly above them, careening down from the top of the slopes, was one of the wooden spools used for storing the metal cables for the ski lifts. Several skiers veered away from the spool as quickly as they could.

"Frank!" Joe yelled. "Get out of the way!"

The giant spool was careening downhill, right for the spot where Ken and Frank stood!

Chapter

2

"RUN FOR IT!" Frank heard Joe yell. Automatically Frank tensed to leap backward out of the spool's speeding path. Then he realized that his feet were still locked into the snowboard bindings, and that they could only be released manually.

Thinking fast, Frank lunged forward with his upper body and shoved Ken out of the spool's path. Ken cried out as he lurched and fell hard, then rolled sideways down the slope.

Frank frantically tried to pivot around on the heel of his board. The spool roared in his ears as it hurtled the last dozen yards toward him.

Just then a pair of strong hands gripped the collar of his parka. Frank felt himself being yanked backward, right off his feet. He landed

11

in a heap on a pile of soft snow just as the giant spool hurtled past.

Looking up, he saw Joe standing over him. "Thanks," Frank said, still shaken. "Boy, talk about close calls. I thought for sure I was a goner that time."

"You would have been, too, if I hadn't been around to save you," Joe said, sounding angry. "Pushing Ken out of the way put you right in front of that thing."

"Is Ken okay?" Frank asked as he rose stiffly to his feet with his brother's help.

Before Joe could answer, the Hardys heard a loud explosion, followed by high-pitched screaming.

Frank turned to see that the huge spool had crashed through the plate-glass window of the restaurant at the base lodge. Broken glass lay in a glittering arc all around the spool. A crowd of skiers and resort staffers was beginning to gather.

Frank pulled a compact pair of binoculars out of his pocket and panned across the wreckage. He saw a waiter examining the crushed remnants of a pastry cart just inside the plate-glass window. "It doesn't look as if anyone down there was hurt," Frank informed Joe. "How about Ken?"

Joe was already bending over the athlete, who was sitting up groggily with a hand to his forehead. Frank moved closer and spotted a thin trickle of blood oozing down from behind Ken's ear.

"Looks as if you banged your head," Frank said. "Better sit quietly for a minute." He took a handkerchief out of his pocket and applied pressure to Ken's wound.

Ken smiled faintly. "Thanks, man. I'll be okay."

"Right," Frank replied. "Hold this tight against that cut and don't move for a few minutes."

Several skiers stopped to see if Ken had been hurt, then continued downhill. Frank joined Joe a few feet away and watched the flocks of curious skiers converging on the base lodge.

"Well, Frank," Joe asked quietly, "what do you think that was all about?"

Frank cast a speculative look at Joe. "I think giant cable spools don't roll down mountainsides by accident."

"Yeah, but why would anyone push it down?" His eyes widened as a thought occurred to him. "You don't think that guy Buck did it, do you?"

"Seems unlikely," Frank admitted, peering up at the slope to where the spool had appeared. "He didn't seem *that* mad. On the other hand, he really wants to beat Ken in the competition tomorrow. And the spool did head right for Ken."

"Hey, what are you guys muttering about?" Ken Gibson called, still pressing the handkerchief to his cut.

"We're going to backtrack up to where that spool came from to look for clues," Frank said. "We think someone might have deliberately pushed that spool."

Gibson's eyes widened in surprise. "Clues?" he asked. "Isn't that a job for the police? You two sound like a couple of detectives."

Frank and Joe exchanged glances. The boys tried to keep their identity a secret when they were with people they didn't know, but it wasn't always possible.

"We're detectives," Frank admitted. "Our dad, Fenton Hardy, is a private investigator in New York. I guess Joe and I are chips off the old block."

"Our track record isn't too bad so far," Joe added. Frank smiled, hearing the excitement in Joe's voice. If there was one thing Joe liked better than snowboarding, it was solving a tough new mystery.

Before Ken had time to comment, they were joined by yet another snowboarder. Frank watched him pop over the hill above them in a spectacular leap, with his legs bent behind him and his snowboard almost touching his arched back.

"Wow," Frank said. He was impressed by how smoothly the lithe, muscular, orange-and-white-clad snowboarder brought his legs into a low crouch and hit the hard-packed slope as lightly as a feather. Next, the agile shredder bent low over his left side, dragging his hand in the

14

snow in a stunning left-hand turn that carried him up to the little group.

Ken Gibson shook his head as a grin spread over his face. "Showing off again, Antonio?"

"Ken, thank goodness you're all right!" the stranger cried in perfect English tinged with a slight Italian accent. "I heard you had an accident."

"Yeah, a freak accident. I was nearly flattened by a runaway cable spool." Ken laughed incredulously, as if he still found it hard to believe. "I'm fine now, though," he added. "Thanks. Meet my friends Frank and Joe Hardy. Guys, this is Antonio Morelli, my number-one opponent in this competition," Gibson said, holding up a hand and high-fiving Morelli.

"Did you two come to Austria to compete?" Morelli asked.

"No," Frank answered. "We're working with security, starting tomorrow. We're not nearly in the same league as you and Ken." He flashed Joe a grin. "Maybe we will be after a few lessons from Ken here."

"So, you're taking on students now?" Morelli asked Ken Gibson.

"Just passing on a few pointers. Or I was till Buck Warburton broke up our lesson," Ken replied.

Morelli made a face. "Yes, that sounds like Buck. Too bad his manners aren't equal to his snowboarding skill."

"Speaking of snowboards, can I ask you

15

about yours, Antonio?" Joe asked. "It looks so much thicker than the ones I've seen. How do you get any flex with it?"

Frank looked closely at the blue and white board and saw that Joe was right. It was over an inch thick.

"Ah! My board is custom-made to my specifications. It's my secret weapon," Morelli replied mischievously. "And with it I'm going to steal the championship from our friend here."

Frank grinned as Ken opened his mouth to make a good-natured retort, but before he could get any words out, a pretty, red-haired skier came zooming down the slope toward them. She stopped on a dime, sending up a spray of loose powder.

"Thanks for the shower," Joe said as he brushed the snow out of his face.

"Whoops! Sorry." She pulled her ski goggles up over the green knit cap she wore over her thick, shoulder-length hair. Her cheeks were flushed from the cold air, and her large green eyes shone with concern. Uh-oh, thought Frank. He knew Joe had a weakness for red-haired girls.

"Hi, Andrea," Ken said, rising to his feet.

"Ken, I heard about the accident. Are you okay?" she asked. Then she saw the cut behind Ken's ear. "What happened to your head?"

"I banged it on a rock when I fell," Ken replied nonchalantly. "I'm okay, thanks to my

16

friends here. Let's see if I can get this right.
Frank saved my life, and Joe saved his brother's."

"Hi, I'm Joe Hardy," Joe said, eagerly taking
her pink-gloved hand. "That's my brother,
Frank."

"Andrea Wells," she told him, shaking hands
with Joe. For an instant her bright, inquisitive
eyes met Joe's interested gaze, and she smiled.

"I was on my way downslope to check out
the damage to the restaurant, but maybe there's
a better story here," she added, peering with
renewed interest at Frank and Joe.

"As it happens, I'm giving interviews tonight
at the lodge," Joe joked. "Would you care to
take a number?"

Before Andrea could shoot back a retort,
Morelli interrupted. "Ken, introduce me to this
beautiful woman. I don't think we've met."

"Andrea, this is my arch-rival, Antonio
Morelli," Gibson complied with a grin. "Andrea
writes for *Shredder* magazine," he added. "You
probably read her stuff."

"Of course!" Morelli's dark eyes lit up. "That
piece on the Cortina meet was excellent. It's a
pleasure to meet you."

"Antonio Morelli?" Andrea looked delighted.
"Oh, of course. I should have recognized you.
What perfect timing! I've been looking for you.
We're putting together a European issue of the
magazine this month, featuring this competition.
I was hoping for an interview."

"I'd be happy to oblige such a lovely American lady," Morelli replied.

"Could I get a picture of you and Ken standing together?" she asked excitedly, taking off her gloves. Frank watched her pull a camera and lens out of a small pack fastened around her waist. "This'll be a great shot with the Alps in the background and both of you holding your boards. Just let me switch to my wide-angle lens."

"What about us?" Frank heard Joe mutter as Andrea quickly arranged her shot. "I thought we were her big scoop of the day."

Frank couldn't resist chuckling at Joe. "Face it, bro," he said as they moved away from the group. "You've been outclassed by a guy who's a mean glider and a smooth talker."

Joe sighed. "She sure is pretty," he said.

Frank smiled. "Yeah, so Morelli noticed. But for now, don't you think we should concentrate on finding out how that spool got loose?"

Joe changed gears instantly, squinting at the sunlight as he peered above them at the top of the slope. "I guess we should ask ourselves why someone would push it down," he reflected. "If it really was aimed at Ken, I guess we'd have to suspect practically everyone in the competition."

"Even Morelli?" Frank looked skeptically at the Italian athlete, who was posing with his arm around Ken's shoulders and a big smile on his face.

"I was thinking about Buck Warburton," Joe

replied. "But now that you mention it, Ken *is* Morelli's stiffest competition."

"It's hard to imagine any of these guys pulling such a dumb stunt, if you ask me," Frank said with a sigh. "But I have to admit, it's got my curiosity up. Why don't we go up and find where the spool was and snoop around?"

He glanced over at Andrea, who was finishing her roll of film. "One more shot," she said to Ken and Antonio. "And put a little hostility into this one, guys. You two have a lot at stake tomorrow."

"Okay," Joe said. "But first let's say goodbye to—"

But Joe never got to finish the sentence. A loud shout shattered the air. Frank turned to see a red and black shape hurtling over the crest of the hill above them. The stocky, muscular form was careening straight at them like a rocket in flight.

"It's Warburton!" Frank shouted. "Hit the ground!"

Chapter

3

INSTANTLY, JOE FELL facedown into the snow. The last thing he saw was Frank pulling Andrea Wells out of Warburton's path. As Joe pressed tightly against the ground, he heard the swooshing sound of Warburton's board passing inches overhead, spraying him with a needlelike shower of tiny ice crystals.

The next instant Joe lifted his head to see Warburton carve a sharp turn back to the group. His wide face was cracked in an evil grin. Joe's temper flared at the sound of his braying laughter.

"What a chicken coop!" Warburton yelled. "You should've seen the way you all scattered. It was priceless."

"You can get kicked off the slopes for that,

Warburton!" Joe shouted as he pushed himself up out of the snow.

"Awww, did I hurt little Junior's feelings?" Buck said in a mocking tone. "Lay off. I was only having some fun."

"You fool, you could've hurt someone," Morelli growled harshly.

"You sure could have," Gibson agreed. "In fact, I ought to report you to the World Snowboarding Congress and have you thrown out of the competition."

To Joe's satisfaction, Warburton immediately dropped his cocky grin and took on a sullen expression. "What's the matter with you guys? Can't you take a joke?"

"Putting people's lives in danger isn't funny," Frank pointed out.

Warburton turned an incredulous gaze on Gibson. "Come on, Ken, you know how good my control is when I'm grabbing air. I wasn't going to hurt anybody. Hey, I missed you all, right?"

"Not by much," Joe said through clenched teeth.

"Why don't we all take a deep breath and relax?" Frank suggested, casting a pointed look in Joe's direction.

"Sure." Gibson gave Warburton a long, hard look. "After Buck apologizes."

"What?" Buck exploded. "But I—"

"Unless," Ken interrupted, "he'd rather sit on the sidelines and cheer for the rest of us tomorrow."

21

"All right." Warburton glared at Gibson. "I'm sorry I scared you."

"Good," Morelli said in a mocking voice. "That was very nice, Buck. Now, why don't you run along and practice some slalom runs. You'll need to practice those soft landings if you don't want to be humiliated at tomorrow's competition."

Warburton glared at Morelli and Gibson as he leaned back on his board and spun the nose around so it pointed downhill. "Wait till tomorrow," he snarled. "We'll see who's humiliated."

As he took off, Andrea Wells perked up, waved goodbye quickly to her companions, and pushed off after him, calling, "Hey, Buck, wait up. I want to talk to you."

"Well, Ken, if I'm going to beat you tomorrow, I'd better get in some practice runs before nightfall," Morelli said wearily. "A pleasure meeting you," he added to Frank and Joe. "Enjoy your stay in Austria."

Joe watched Morelli whiz downhill and said, "He's some shredder."

"You bet," Gibson replied. "He'll give me some stiff competition this week."

"What about Warburton?" Joe asked, turning back to face Ken and Frank.

Gibson shrugged. "If he doesn't get a handle on his temper, he'll stay small-time forever. I'm not worried about him."

Ken's attention was caught by something uphill.

Joe followed his gaze and spotted a female snow-boarder bearing down on them at high speed.

As she drew closer, Joe eyed her graceful movements and her long, billowing, ash blond hair. She braked expertly right at Gibson's feet, then smoothly leaned over to plant a kiss on his lips.

Joe laughed in surprise. The new boarder was quite beautiful, despite the fact that her nose was a little crooked, as though it had been broken and badly set. She looked a little older than Ken, and when she spoke, it was with a Russian accent.

"Ken, where have you been?" she demanded. "I was worried about you."

"Oh, just talking shop." Gibson winked at Frank and Joe. "Ivana Garova, meet Frank and Joe Hardy. Ivana's one of the judges at the competition," he added.

Joe and Frank shook hands with her, but Ivana looked distracted. "Guys, I have to speak to Kenny in private for a second. Would you please excuse us?"

"No problem," Joe said. "We were just going upslope for some practice runs."

"Thanks again, Frank and Joe," Ken said. "I sure am glad I ran into you today."

Joe laughed and waved goodbye as he and Frank pushed off.

As soon as they were far enough away from Ken and Ivana to avoid being overheard, Joe turned to Frank and said, "Let's go check out the spot where the cable spool came from. I'm afraid all the skiers may have erased any clues by now."

Frank agreed. "I doubt we'll find anything. But it beats standing around here getting cold."

It took only a few moments for Joe and Frank to glide downslope to the gondola that would take them up to the top of the run. They unfastened their bindings and climbed into the red gondola, holding their boards up against their bodies to make room for the other skiers who crowded in after them.

On the way up Joe gazed out the gondola's open window at the jagged range of mountains that ringed the resort. The sight of scores of colorful skiers and snowboarders whizzing among the peaks and the feel of the cold winter air in his face were exciting.

"I'm afraid there's not much chance of any evidence going undisturbed in this crowd," Frank said to his brother.

"You may be right, Frank," Joe answered, "but so what? This view has been worth the ride."

After getting off the gondola, Joe and Frank quickly snapped their boots into their bindings, and then, starting off with little hops into the air, they set out to find the place where the spool had come from. Joe spotted its double tracks leading from a steel column halfway up the advanced ski slope. The column supported a

24

closed-down chair lift adjacent to the gondola the Hardys had just used.

When they reached the column, though, Joe's heart sank. The spot was overrun with several teenage ski-lift operators, a couple of workmen who seemed to be trying to repair the lift, and a handful of curious skiers.

Joe and Frank dismounted their boards and moved closer to the workmen. They were talking German, prompting Joe to lean over to Frank and whisper, "Now would be a good time to use your new electronic gizmo."

Joe watched as Frank pulled out his new pocket translator. Frank had insisted on buying it the moment he learned they were flying to Austria, though it had cost him two hundred dollars.

Joe shook his head, amused at Frank's weakness for electronic gadgets. He waited as Frank listened intently, his fingers flying across the palm-size keyboard. About half the size of a paperback book, the device could not only translate English words into six languages, including German, but it could also translate foreign words into English if approximate spellings were typed in.

Joe took a quick look at the area surrounding the support pole. To his disappointment, the snow had been thoroughly trampled. Any footprints or other clues had probably been erased.

Joe turned back to Frank and tried to read the

translation on the computer screen. "Find out anything?"

"The workmen keep insisting that they left wooden wedges under the spool. The foreman says it couldn't possibly have rolled free by itself."

"Then who pushed it?" Joe asked pointedly.

"That's the mystery," Frank replied. "These guys don't know. They were at the employees' lounge on a coffee break."

"Do you think we should question them?" Joe asked.

Frank shook his head. "No. We don't look like officials or anything. Besides, I doubt we'd learn any more, and if we talk to them, word might get back to the real culprit that we're on his or her trail."

"That reminds me. We ought to find Ken and ask him to keep quiet about who we are," Joe suggested.

Joe scanned the slopes below for Ken Gibson. He finally spotted him, still standing with Ivana Garova. Though the pair were at least two hundred yards away, Joe could tell they were arguing. Garova was walking in a circle around Gibson, making angry gestures. Then she turned toward him and stamped her foot.

I wonder what that's all about, Joe thought to himself as he and Frank zoomed toward Gibson and Garova. The closer they got, the angrier Ivana looked. When they were about fifty yards from the couple, Joe saw Ivana slap Ken Gibson across the face. Then she strapped her snow-board onto her boots and whizzed off.

Gibson looked over at the Hardys when they arrived. "Did we come at a bad time, Ken?" Frank asked.

Ken sighed. "No, I'm okay."

"Uh, we don't mean to intrude," Joe said sympathetically. "Do you want to be alone?"

Gibson shook his head. "No. In fact, I was wondering if you guys could come with me back to the lodge. I could use the company."

Ten minutes later Ken Gibson was leading the Hardys through the cheery, wood-paneled halls of the resort's main lodge. "Let's go up to my room. I'll have room service send up some hot drinks and sandwiches," Gibson said as he led them to the elevator.

Moments later the three snowboarders arrived at the door to Ken's room. Ken wearily unlocked the door, and the Hardys followed him into the darkened room.

"Ow!" Joe said as he banged his shin on a suitcase. "Could you put on a light, Ken? I can't see anything."

"Sorry," Gibson replied, going over to his bedside table. "These rooms on the east side get really dark around sunset."

Gibson turned to Frank and Joe as he reached for the metal chain that turned on his bedside lamp. "Oh, what kind of sandwiches do you—"

The rest of Gibson's sentence was cut off as an explosion erupted from the bedside lamp. Joe stared in disbelief as flames leaped across the table and bed.

Joe and Frank watched, horrified, as Ken let out a piercing scream and raced from the room. His upper body was becoming engulfed in rapidly spreading flames!

Chapter

4

"KEN!" FRANK SHOUTED as he and Joe leaped into action.

"Joe, stop him!" Frank grabbed a heavy blanket off the foot of the bed.

"Ahhh!" Gibson screamed. He whirled around in a frantic circle just outside the doorway to his room as the flames spread on his jacket.

Joe ran into the hallway and yanked off his own jacket. Then he tackled Ken, knocking him to the ground as Frank threw the blanket over him. Together the brothers rolled Ken in the blanket, using their gloved hands and Joe's jacket to help smother the flames.

"Joe—there's a fire extinguisher down the hall. Get it, quick!" Frank directed.

Joe turned on his heel and sped away while

Frank continued beating at the flames. A moment later Gibson's burning jacket was extinguished, though the bedside table and bed inside the room still burned furiously.

As Frank dragged the stunned Gibson farther away from the flames, Joe used the red fire extinguisher to spray the base of the fire. In less than a minute Joe had the fire out. A thick pall of smoke hung in the room, making him cough. After setting the fire extinguisher down, Joe threw open the room's wide windows to let the smoke out.

Out in the hall Frank unwrapped the blanket from around Gibson. To his relief, Gibson's eyes were open and his face looked unscathed.

"Ken, are you all right?" Frank asked urgently.

Coughing, Gibson shook his head up and down.

"How badly are you burned?" Frank persisted.

"J-just my hand, I think," Gibson managed to gasp. "Help me get this parka off so I can see how bad the burn is."

"No. Keep it on. The doctors can cut it off at the hospital," Frank instructed. "The nylon might have melted to your skin. We can't risk tearing it."

"That's two I owe you," Gibson said weakly.

"Don't worry about that," Frank said. "Just lie back. Joe, go call an ambulance. I'll stay here with Ken."

"Right." Joe stepped around Ken and Frank and sprinted down the hall toward the elevator.

Why would someone have done this? Frank wondered, watching Joe go. At any rate, it seemed clear now that the incident on the slopes earlier had been no accident. Someone really was after Ken Gibson. But who, and what for?

Just then Frank noticed that the door of one of the rooms down the hall was slightly ajar. His eyes met those of the person behind the door for just a moment, but that moment was long enough. The face behind the door was Buck Warburton's.

Frank awoke the next morning feeling tired. He and Joe had accompanied Ken Gibson to the emergency room, where he had been treated for first-degree burns to his left hand. Frank was thankful that his and Joe's quick actions had saved Gibson from further injury.

Sitting up in bed, Frank wearily recalled the two hours he and Joe had spent explaining to a plump Austrian police inspector named Kempf how Gibson had gotten burned. In the tradition of small-town policemen the world over, Kempf had been methodical and maddeningly slow. Both Frank and Joe were vastly relieved to finally leave the Graz police station sometime after midnight. Frank remembered how hard it had been to keep his eyes open during the taxi ride back up the mountain to the lodge.

Sighing, Frank reached over to shake his

brother awake. "Up and at 'em, soldier," he bellowed, throwing on a pair of jeans. "It's World Championship day!"

Half an hour later Frank and Joe were wolfing down scrambled eggs and cinnamon-covered pastries in the enormous basement dining room, their snowboards on the floor beside them.

"Fifteen more minutes," Frank warned, gulping down his orange juice. "Then we report for duty as crowd-control marshals at the unparalleled World Snowboarding Championships."

"I've been thinking about the explosion in Ken's room last night," Joe remarked, ignoring the warning as he reached for another pastry.

"Yeah, and?" Frank prompted.

"I still don't understand how it worked," Joe said.

Frank finished off his juice. "I think I know. Gibson's assailant must have filled a light bulb with gasoline. It blew up as soon as the electric current ran through it and sparked."

Joe grinned appreciatively. "Good theory. The gasoline would explain why the flames spread so fast and burned so fiercely. But how do you fill a light bulb with gasoline without breaking it?"

"Simple. You use a syringe with a narrow-gauge needle to inject the gasoline through the base of the bulb."

"That sounds like it would work all right," Joe agreed. "How'd you think of that?"

Frank shrugged. "I saw it in a movie."

Joe laughed. "Okay, we have the method now, but still no motive. Who would want Ken Gibson dead, and why?"

"You've got me. Right now we really don't know enough about Ken to do more than guess."

"Then my guess is that someone is trying to take him out of the snowboarding competition before it starts," Joe offered.

"If that's so, then Warburton's a likely suspect. I told you how I noticed him lurking in one of the doorways last night," Frank pointed out.

"Yeah, but we saw Warburton go into Kempf's office last night at the police station right after he grilled us. If Kempf let him go, he must have been satisfied with Warburton's explanation."

"What about Ivana Garova?" Frank suggested. "That little scene we saw on the slopes yesterday was pretty ugly. Ken didn't say what the argument was about. You think Ivana could have thought it was worth killing him over?"

Joe looked skeptical. "There's Morelli, too," he said. "He was the first to show up after the spool incident, so he's a suspect, too. But without more info about Ken's past, we're just shooting in the dark," Joe added.

Frank clapped his brother on the shoulder. "Come on, Joe, think. You were reading all the snowboarding mags before we left. You must have learned something about Gibson. He's a top competitor. Maybe you can come up with some detail that might give us a clue."

Joe thought for a moment. "Well, Gibson

used to be on the pro skiing circuit. He started when he was still in high school. I think he's from Denver or somewhere around there."

"Keep going," Frank prompted, glancing around at the other diners to make sure no one was listening.

"I know he went to Northern Arizona University on an ROTC scholarship and then went into the army for three years, because he didn't compete much during that period. Now he snowboards professionally. He makes his living off prize money and product endorsements. Oh, and I think he picks up a few bucks giving boarding lessons at some resorts in the States. That's all I can remember," Joe finished.

"At least it gives us somewhere to start," Frank said. He paused for a moment, deep in thought. "We could use some background information here. I brought my laptop computer, but it's going to be hard to tap in to the datanet from over here."

"Maybe we should ask Dad to do some checks for us," Joe suggested.

"You read my mind," Frank replied. "We'll ask him to check on Warburton, Garova, and Morelli, just to cover all bases. Let's run a check on Ken, too. Maybe there's more at stake here than just a championship."

"In the meantime, I think one of us should stick close to Ken until we know who we're up against," Frank suggested.

Frank glanced at the clock above the cash register. "Drink up, Joe. We have just enough time to send a fax to Dad before we meet Herr Skopp to get our security assignments."

"You know, Frank," Joe said as they headed through the door, "with all these attempts on Ken's life, it seems like a waste of time working security at the competition. I'd rather be solving this case."

"I know what you mean," Frank agreed. "But a deal's a deal. Besides, working security will let us go behind the scenes at the competition. That should help our investigation."

"Let's hope it does," Joe said. "We can use all the help we can get."

After sending their father a fax the Hardys headed outside to receive their security assignments. Despite the early hour, Frank and Joe saw that the resort was already a whirl of activity as they found the security trailer and introduced themselves to Heinrich Skopp, the competition's Austrian security chief.

"Welcome to Graz," Skopp said briskly in crisp, unaccented English. "I don't anticipate any problems today, but if you need help, let me know. I have here your walkie-talkies, security passes for you to wear around your necks, and these orange armbands."

Skopp assigned Joe to a four-man security crew responsible for roping off a clear area for the press and assuring that the network film crews had an undisturbed view of the action.

Frank's job was to direct the hordes of spectators into roped-off areas overlooking the advanced ski slope.

Once Frank got into the rhythm of his job, he began to take in more of what was going on around him. He noted the course the competitors were to use: a steep, zigzagging trail dotted with small red flags that the snowboarders would have to slalom around. Frank remembered from the schedule that tomorrow's events were the giant slalom and halfpipe acrobatic competitions.

Today's competition, however, was a combination of slalom racing with a halfpipe near the end of the course for acrobatics. The racers would have to negotiate all of the slalom turns on the course or they would be disqualified. But the highlight of the course would be the halfpipe: a jump ramp carved into the earth right at the mouth of a deep crevasse that ran from above the racecourse nearly down to the finish line.

From where he stood, midway down the course, Frank could see the starting gate about a thousand feet away, and the finish line. He could also see the judges' booth, a covered wooden box with an open front that could seat three people, parallel to the finish line. The judges, including Ivana Garova, were already in place.

Frank heard a rousing cheer ripple through the crowd as the competitors appeared at the base of the slope. There they climbed aboard the gondola that would take them up to the starting gate. When Ken Gibson appeared in a red, white, and blue ski suit with the number seven on the front and back, an even bigger cheer went up. He had drawn many American fans to the event.

Ken looked up the slope. His keen eyes picked Frank out of the crowd, and he gave him a quick thumbs-up. Frank grinned and responded with a thumbs-up gesture of his own. Then he saw Ken wave to Ivana Garova, who quickly looked away. Frank peered through his binoculars to gauge Ken's reaction to this snub. He looks pretty discouraged, Frank thought. I wonder what's really happening with those two.

Using the binoculars, he turned his attention to the press area farther down the slope, where Joe was working. He noticed Andrea Wells, dressed in a white ski suit trimmed with red. She held a camera with a long telephoto lens and was staring at Garova with a curious expression. Frank guessed that she, too, had seen Garova snub Gibson. He made a mental note to ask Andrea what she knew about the couple's relationship.

A few moments later loudspeakers all around the course crackled, and a male voice speaking first in German, then in French, Italian, and English, welcomed the fans and competitors to the annual World Snowboarding Association Championships.

Even without the English translation, Frank recognized Ken Gibson's name as the first competitor. "Go, Ken!" he cheered along with the rest of the crowd, beating his gloves together as hard as he could.

Frank brought his binoculars to bear on Gibson just as the athlete approached the starting gate. At the starter's signal Gibson hopped up into the air, raising his board several inches off the ground. The bottom of the board hit the snow, and he was rocketing downhill at breathtaking speed.

"Man, he must be going sixty miles an hour," Frank said to himself, marveling at Gibson's grace and total control of the board. "I hope he doesn't knock that burned hand on anything."

Gibson covered the course like the champion he was. Then he approached the halfpipe jump ramp. As he slid closer toward it, Frank heard four small popping sounds. He peered through his binoculars at Ken, but Gibson apparently didn't hear the noise. His speed increased just before he disappeared behind the walls of the halfpipe near the end of the crevasse.

As Frank waited for Ken to reappear, he heard an ominous rumble that seemed to be coming from up the mountain. The rumbling noise quickly grew in volume. Frank felt a vibration beneath his feet.

In a flash Frank realized what was happening. "Avalanche!" he yelled, dropping his binoculars and staring at the crevasse, where a mass of snow was bearing down with unbelievable force and speed. The avalanche was going to bury Ken Gibson!

Chapter

5

DOWN AT THE END of the course by the press area, Joe heard a muffled boom and looked up in surprise. A white wall of snow was pouring down the long crevasse toward the bottom of the mountain. It was headed straight for the half-pipe, where Ken Gibson was completing his performance! It was obvious that he was traveling too fast to notice the avalanche. Joe tried to think fast. There was no way to warn him in time.

As the reporters and camera crews nearby started to scream and shout, Joe turned to one of the video monitors with a sick feeling in his stomach. Only luck could save Ken Gibson now.

As Gibson entered the halfpipe, he crouched atop his speeding snowboard in preparation for his acrobatic jump. The next second the roaring torrent of snow came pouring down into the half-pipe. Joe watched helplessly as Ken's brightly clad form vanished under the crushing weight of the swiftly moving snow.

Gibson had disappeared, and the dip in the racecourse was filled with snow. Joe heard a frightened, agitated babble of voices all around him.

There were only brief moments to spare, and Joe leaped into action. He vaulted the barricade around the press area and poured on the speed as he headed for the halfpipe about a hundred yards away.

Competition staff and panicked spectators were starting to run out onto the flat area at the base of the course. Here's one advantage of being a football player, Joe thought as he used every-thing he knew about broken field running to get across the area fast. Another member of the security staff tried to wave Joe away, but he dodged left and slipped right past him.

Seconds later Joe scrambled up the barrier that formed one side of the halfpipe. Inside, the halfpipe looked like a level field of snow, and Joe's heart sank.

Suddenly Joe saw something sticking out of the snow. It was bright red. Maybe it was part of Ken's board, Joe hoped as he started to run for it, sinking in the loose snow up to his knees. Lifting his feet as high as he could, he reached the spot and swept away an armful of snow. It *was* Ken's board!

Joe started digging frantically in the snow with his hands. He knew it would be blind luck if he could find Ken in time, but he had to try.

He worked around the board in widening circles, kicking his feet and swinging his arms through the snow. Suddenly his fingers brushed something round and smooth. He dropped to his knees and started digging desperately. It was Ken's red, white, and blue helmet.

Working fast, he cleared the area all around the helmet and in one sweeping armful uncovered Ken's face. The athlete's eyes were closed. He didn't seem to be breathing. Thinking quickly, Joe reached down and unfastened the helmet's chin strap.

At that moment Ken's mouth opened, and Joe heard him gasp as his lungs sucked in the freezing air. Ken's eyelids fluttered briefly but didn't open.

Greatly relieved, Joe reached for the walkie-talkie in its holster on his hip and thumbed the call button. "Emergency, this is a priority call! I've located Gibson! Over."

"On our way now," a voice came crackling back. "Stay with him."

Joe rushed to the side of the halfpipe, looked over, and saw a big Sno-Cat. The large vehicle, mounted on tank treads, was headed for him. He waved his arms over his head, and the Sno-

Cat flashed its headlights to signal that he'd been spotted.

Reassured, Joe returned to Ken and found that he was still breathing shallowly. Only his face and helmet showed above the snow.

"Okay, we've got him," said a rescue worker behind Joe as several medics came pouring over the edge of the halfpipe and set to work with frantic haste. Joe helped them transfer a stretcher, thermal blankets, and several braces to Gibson's side.

"Good work, kid," one of the medics said to Joe. "I haven't seen running like that since the Super Bowl."

"Is he going to be okay?" Joe asked.

"Well, you found him before he suffocated," the medic replied. "But we're going to have to unbury him carefully. We have to put braces on his neck and back before we can risk moving him."

Joe's walkie-talkie crackled, and he heard Frank's voice. "Calling Joe Hardy, over."

"I'm here, Frank. Ken's alive. Over."

"Great! I'm headed your way on a snowmobile. Be outside the press area in five minutes. Over and out."

Ten minutes later Joe was hanging on to the rear seat handles of a powerful snowmobile and straining to catch Frank's words over the roar of the engine.

"Whoever Gibson's enemies are, they almost got him with that avalanche!" Frank shouted.

"There's no way that was a coincidence. Did you hear a series of small popping sounds just before it hit?"

"No!" Joe hollered, squinting his eyes against the cold mountain wind. "I was too far away."

Frank looked over his shoulder at his younger brother. "If my theory is correct, we'll find some kind of explosive or detonator at the top of the crevasse."

"Great. But, Frank," Joe said suddenly, "couldn't the noise from this snowmobile set off another avalanche?"

"That's a possibility," Frank replied over the engine's roar. "If any more of this snow starts sliding, we're going to be in a tight spot."

Moving carefully but swiftly, Frank guided the blue and silver snowmobile over the heaps of snow to the top of the crevasse. Frank throttled down as he pulled into a natural amphitheater formed by a thick wall of tall pine trees lining a jumble of huge granite boulders.

"Looks as if more than one person has been here recently," Frank said, observing several snowmobile tracks in the snow.

"Let me use your binoculars," Joe asked. With the glasses in one hand, Joe scrambled up onto one of the big boulders and focused on the action on the racecourse below. He was far to the side of the course, but Joe still had an unobstructed view of the area around the halfpipe and finish line.

"What's going on?" Frank asked, concerned. "Have they gotten him out yet?"

Joe studied the rescue team's movements. "They're still digging around his legs," he said.

Joe turned to Frank and saw his brother staring fixedly at the side of the mountain. "What do you see, Frank?"

Frank paused a moment, gazing above and below them. "From what I know about avalanches, they usually carry tons of snow and can travel up to a couple of miles," Frank murmured. "This one petered out in less than half a mile."

"Yeah? And?" Joe prompted.

"And avalanches occur most often when a lot of heavy snow builds up, or when the sun is shining on a big field of snow." Frank pointed up to the top of the crevasse. "But that area is in the shade until at least late afternoon."

"That makes sense to me." Joe nodded. His expression turned grim. "So we're looking for some type of explosive? I didn't hear a loud bang or anything."

"But there were those popping sounds," Frank reminded him. "Even a small charge can set off a reaction in an unstable mass like snow if it's placed correctly."

"Okay, Einstein," Joe said with a sigh. "Let's start at the top of that ridge in the center. We can cover more ground if we split up."

Fifteen minutes later Joe was starting to feel cold. I'd give my life savings for a thermos of hot chocolate, he thought to himself. Every few minutes he paused in his search to peer down at the rescue team. He could just make out a form clad in red, white, and blue lying still on the snow. I'm going to find out who did this to Ken, he swore to himself, turning back to his search with renewed vigor.

A moment later Joe found his first clue. It was a footprint. Following the direction it pointed, he found more prints, leading to a tall spruce tree. Brushing some loose snow away from the base of the tree, Joe suddenly spotted a bright red wire.

"Hey, Frank," Joe hollered to his brother. "Get over here on the double. I think I've found something."

Frank waved his arms to signal that he'd heard and began to cautiously make his way across the slippery snow.

Joe bent down and tugged gently at the bit of red wire lying on top of the snow. Dusting away snow as he went, he followed the wire to a spot just behind one of the big granite boulders. The wire ran into a small green metal box with a twelve-inch whip antenna. As he examined it, he heard Frank come up behind him.

"This must be the detonator," Joe said excitedly. "We were right, Frank. What happened to Ken was no accident."

Frank looked thoughtful. "Don't touch anything else, Joe. I'm going to radio Herr Skopp and have him contact Inspector Kempf."

"Hey, look at this," Joe said. "On the other side of this box, isn't that Russian lettering?"

Frank peered closely at the detonator. "I think you're right, Joe. This clue could point to Ivana. But what motive she could have to do something like this completely stumps me."

Frank dug into his small backpack and pulled out his camera. He quickly photographed the detonator box from several angles, being careful to get pictures of the detonator's serial number.

Joe noticed his brother's thoroughness with approval. "Good idea. We can use the serial number to trace the detonator." He watched Frank stow his camera, grab his walkie-talkie, and try to raise Herr Skopp on it.

Joe tapped his brother on the shoulder. "You know, Frank, if Skopp calls Kempf and Kempf finds us up here, he's going to keep us busy for hours questioning us."

"I know that," Frank replied seriously. "We don't have time to be questioned. We've got to move fast on this new clue."

"I say we radio in directions to this place and then split," Joe suggested. "We'll talk to Kempf all he wants once this mystery is solved."

Frank was about to agree, but just then a shriek cut the air directly above the Hardys' heads. Instinctively Frank and Joe leaped backward. Looking up, they saw the huge branch of a nearby pine tree come crashing down toward them!

Chapter

6

FRANK DIVED FOR COVER, landing face first in a huge snowbank as the branch landed where he'd been standing only a second before. Leaping to his feet and spinning around, he saw a flash of bright green and pink under the fallen limb. Suddenly Andrea Wells's face popped up from behind a spray of pine needles. "Hi, guys," she said, climbing out gingerly from her fallen perch. "Uh, fancy meeting you here."

"What were you doing up in that tree?" Joe asked, looking surprised and perplexed as he rushed to help her to her feet. "Are you injured?"

"No, I'm okay," she replied, embarrassed. "I came up here by snowmobile to get some telephoto shots of the rescue, but I guess I've found out more than I bargained for. I heard you guys talking about the detonator. What are you two, some kind of detectives?''

"I hope you don't plan to write about this," Frank replied with a worried scowl. "As a reporter, you should know that any media coverage now could foul up our investigation."

"Of course I intend to write about it! I'm a reporter, remember? So tell me, you think somebody tried to kill Ken Gibson on purpose?''

She looked from one silent brother to the other. It was obvious that neither one intended to speak. "Okay, we can make a deal here," Andrea offered. "You give me an exclusive on this story, and I swear I won't breathe a word to anyone until you've solved the case."

Frank looked at Joe, who reluctantly nodded.

"Okay," Frank replied seriously. "The exclusive is yours, and maybe you can be of some help in the investigation. But meanwhile, not a word to anyone."

"Agreed," Andrea replied with a smile. "Hey, look," she said suddenly, pointing down at the racecourse. "They're bringing Ken down."

Frank took his binoculars from Joe and peered down at the big Sno-Cat pulling out of the crevasse below them. He could see Gibson's body lashed to a stretcher, which two medics hurried over to a waiting ambulance. Another medic ran along with the stretcher, hovering over Gibson.

"Guys, I'm going down to see how badly Ken's hurt," Andrea said. "I'll catch you later—and I won't blow your cover. But don't forget, you owe me!'' Andrea ran toward a snowmobile concealed behind a large boulder. ''Meet me at the base lodge restaurant,'' she called over her shoulder as she sped away.

''We owe *her?''* Joe muttered, confused.

''Forget Andrea. Let's concentrate on the case,'' Frank said. ''We need to pin Morelli down on exactly where he was when that spool broke loose.''

''I'm for that,'' Joe replied as he jumped aboard their snowmobile and revved it up. ''I'll have us there in no time.''

Half an hour later, in the hall outside Morelli's room, Frank could hear what sounded like one side of a heated argument being carried on in Italian. He guessed that Morelli was talking on the phone. Quickly pulling out his pocket translator, Frank started hitting keys as fast as he could.

''I don't know yet . . . definitely alive . . . yes, alive . . . I'll check on that. . . . Ciao.''

When the conversation was over, Frank waited a few moments and knocked on the door. There was no reply. Frank and Joe exchanged glances.

''Morelli, open up.'' Joe banged loudly on the door. ''It's Joe and Frank Hardy.''

The door opened a crack, and Morelli peered out at them.

''Hello, boys,'' Morelli said. ''Sorry. I was on the telephone. What do you want?''

Now that Frank was face-to-face with the mild-mannered Morelli, he wasn't sure how to begin. "We were wondering if you'd heard anything about Ken Gibson's condition," Frank said, thinking quickly.

Morelli shook his head. "You two probably know as much as I do."

Trying to draw Morelli out, Joe commented, "Some of the stuff that's happened to Ken is downright weird, don't you think?

"What do you mean?" Morelli asked, sounding puzzled.

"Well, we were curious about how that cable spool rolled downhill by itself yesterday, so Frank and I went up to the spot where it came from," Joe told Morelli.

"I overheard the workmen up there say there was no way that spool could have gotten loose by accident," Frank added. He closely observed Morelli's reaction, hoping to startle Morelli into betraying some guilt.

But the Italian's face was a bland mask as he replied, "Indeed? That *is* strange. Perhaps it was an act of vandalism."

"Maybe. And maybe it was something else," Joe said pointedly, also studying Morelli's reaction.

There was a moment of silence, then Morelli said, "Well, all this excitement has worn me out. I think I'll take a nap. I want to be well rested when the competition resumes in a couple of days."

"A couple of days?" Frank asked in surprise.

"Yes, the competition has been delayed while the resort staff regrooms the slopes. They want to be sure there won't be any more avalanches." He reached for the door handle. "Now, if you'll excuse me . . ."

"Say, did you notice—" Joe began, but his words were cut off by the click of the closing door. "Well, I guess that's the end of that conversation," he muttered.

"For someone who claims he's Ken Gibson's friend," Frank said as he and his brother headed down the hall, "Morelli sure doesn't seem very concerned about him."

"No, he doesn't," Joe replied. "Let's head over to the restaurant and meet Andrea."

Frank followed his younger brother across the resort's upstairs restaurant to Andrea's table. The wide, sunlit room was filled with skiers and boarders, media people and spectators from the snowboarding competition. Joe and Frank overheard a reporter say that no word was out on Ken's condition, as he was still in the emergency room.

"Look at that," Joe remarked to his brother.

Frank followed his gaze, seeing that the atrium at the end of the room had been roped off and the smashed windows covered in sheets of clear plastic.

Frank and Joe both ordered sandwiches and sodas and finished them off quickly as Andrea told them about the spectators' horrified reactions to the avalanche.

"I'm going to get a great story out of this," Andrea said as she ate her chef's salad. "And on top of everything, I never would have pegged you two as detectives."

"That's what makes a good detective," Joe replied. "Blending in with the scenery is a great way to pick up information."

"But enough bragging," Frank said, quickly avoiding Joe's quick kick under the table. "Andrea, could I ask you to develop those photos I took of the detonator?"

"Sure, Frank," she replied. "It'll take an hour or so. And I'm going to see my friend Marcy, who works for the Sports Network video crew, to get a videotape of Ken's run."

"Hey, could you get us a copy of that tape?" Frank asked eagerly. "That might be just what we need to crack this case."

"No problem!" Andrea said, rising and pulling on her bright green parka. "Call me at Room three-oh-three about two-thirty. I should have everything you need."

Frank gave her the roll of film, and she left the restaurant.

"Well, Frank, what do you think our next move should be?" Joe asked.

"We have three suspects—Ivana, Warburton, and Morelli—but no clear motive," Frank replied. "At first I thought the motive was either professional jealousy or a lovers' spat, but the incidents with the light bulb and the avalanche suggest there might be something bigger at stake.''

"Then we have to find out what it is about Gibson that should make someone try to kill him," Joe decided.

"I agree." Frank signaled to the waitress for the check. "That's why I want to get the background information on Ken and the suspects from Dad before we do anything else."

Back in the Hardys' room it took Frank only a few minutes to hook his computer's modem up to the hotel's phone line. Getting through to his father took a lot longer. After several frustrating minutes he heard his father's hearty voice on the other end of the line.

"How's it going, son?" Fenton Hardy inquired.

"Couldn't be better, Dad," Frank replied. "But we need those background checks. Do you have them?"

"Yes. Is your computer on line?" Fenton asked.

"All booted up and ready to go," Frank replied.

"I'm sending you the Interpol file and a police record on Buck Warburton from here in the States. He sounds like a real thug, Frank. Be careful around him," Fenton warned.

"We're being careful, Dad," Frank said. "Did you find anything on Ken Gibson?"

"Just standard background information. Nothing to arouse any suspicions," Fenton answered.

"Anything on Garova or Morelli?"

"No criminal records on Morelli," Fenton told him. "Since Garova's Russian, I could only come up with background from the years since she left Russia. I've got a friend in the State Department looking into her earlier history, but that will take a day or two. Turn on your modem, and I'll send you what I've got."

"Thanks, Dad. Tell Mom we say hi."

Frank flicked on the modem's switch, and it hummed to life. Frank's computer printer quickly spat out a dozen sheets, detailing Buck Warburton's U.S. arrest record, a two-page Interpol file, and then brief files on Ken Gibson and Ivana Garova.

Frank rapidly scanned the printouts, searching for anything that would offer a clue to the attacks on Ken Gibson. As he finished each sheet, he handed them to Joe, who also studied them intently.

"Well, except for Warburton's arrests for assault, and Interpol's note that he hangs out with European gangsters, there's not much here to explain the attempts on Ken's life," Frank said gloomily a short time later.

"You're right," Joe agreed. "There's nothing interesting in the files on Ken and Ivana."

"Then let's see what we can turn up in Ken's room," Frank said. "I know it's a long shot, but we have to find out if there's a good reason for someone to want to kill him."

"Good idea. The hotel manager moved him to Room two-oh-one after the fire, so I guess that's our next stop," Joe suggested.

Fifteen minutes later Joe stood in the hall outside Gibson's room chatting with a hotel maid who spoke broken English. Moving as quietly as he could, Frank tiptoed up behind her and snitched the master room key from her cart of cleaning supplies. He deftly opened Gibson's door, replaced the key on the maid's cart, and slipped into the room. Then he drew the window shades and turned on a dim light. A moment later he heard Joe's rap on the door and opened it a crack to let him in.

Frank surveyed the pile of luggage and snowboarding gear in the center of the room. "Looks as if Ken didn't have time to unpack after he moved in here. You take one side of this pile, and I'll take the other."

The Hardys carefully opened Ken's suitcases and began sifting through their contents. The first suitcase Frank opened held only clothes and a few snowboarding magazines. Frank began sifting through Gibson's collection of helmets, gloves, kneepads, and other safety gear.

Finally Frank spied a small leather briefcase and pulled it from the pile. It was locked. Frank pulled a slim steel lockpick from his wallet and opened the lock.

"This looks more interesting," Frank murmured as he paged through Gibson's passport, a sheaf of traveler's checks, a small atlas of Europe, and a well-thumbed German-English dictionary. Then his attention was grabbed by a bundle of letters. Frank opened the bundle and saw from the return address that they were all from Ivana.

Frank flipped quickly through the letters, but he found nothing of interest, except that one of the later letters referred to an upcoming marriage between Ivana and Ken. He looked over at Joe and saw him shaking something.

"I just hit the jackpot," Joe whispered excitedly, waving his brother over to his side. Joe held up Gibson's battered shaving kit. "This thing's got a secret compartment."

"How can you tell?" Frank asked eagerly.

"When I emptied it out, it still felt too heavy," Joe replied. "And I think I hear something moving when I shake it."

Frank watched as Joe took out his pocketknife and carefully pried up the vinyl bag's square bottom plate.

"Bingo," Joe whispered. He turned the bag over and dumped the contents out onto the floor.

It was a small notebook. Frank started leafing through the pages, which were filled with handwritten notes, while Joe lifted a small overnight bag up to his ear and shook it. "What's up?" Frank asked.

"I think there's something concealed in this bag, too. Maybe sewn inside," Joe replied

56

thoughtfully. "I just can't figure out how to get it out."

"Keep working on it while I see what's in this notebook," Frank said.

Frank scanned the notebook's first page again. Gibson had written a cryptic note that said only, Warburton and European gangsters.

Intrigued, Frank turned to the next page. It read, "Is Ivana involved? Blackmail by KGB?"

Frank looked over to tell Joe what he'd found and saw Joe's eyes widen in surprise.

"Take a look at this!" Joe exclaimed.

He pulled his hand out of the overnight bag. It held a .45 automatic pistol.

Chapter

7

"SOMETHING'S FISHY around here, bro." Joe examined the compact, deadly looking .45 automatic before handing it over to Frank.

"So Ken Gibson packs a pistol," Frank said thoughtfully. "That's a surprise, but it doesn't tell us who tried to knock him off."

"I have a hunch who it might be," Joe said. "Warburton's the first person mentioned in that notebook of Ken's."

"Let's not jump to any conclusions," Frank said as he copied Gibson's notes into his own notebook. "We don't even know what the notebook's for yet. And Ken's notes imply that Ivana could be involved with the KGB."

"That's not going to be easy to research," Joe said as he continued examining Gibson's overnight bag. Joe dug his fingers farther into the compartment and found something soft wedged in the back.

Joe was surprised to see that it was a black ankle holster made of black leather. "Look at this. It's like the one Dad wears for his undercover work."

Joe saw Frank's eyes narrow thoughtfully. 'If he's carrying this gun concealed, maybe Ken's some kind of undercover agent," Frank suggested.

"That makes sense," Joe agreed. "Especially since those notes refer to gangsters and the KGB. And maybe the person Ken was spying on tried to kill him."

"My thoughts exactly," Frank said, handing the notebook back to Joe. "Now, let's pack this stuff up and get out of here."

Joe nodded, but as he tried to slip the notebook back into its hiding place, he found that something was in the way. Joe probed around with a finger and touched a folded piece of paper. Curious, he drew it out and unfolded it. It looked like an ordinary Swiss franc note.

"Frank, check this out," Joe said.

Frank looked it over, then handed it back with a puzzled expression. "It's a twenty-franc note. So what?"

"Why was it in the secret compartment?" Joe wondered.

"Maybe we should hang on to this bill until we find out what makes it so special," Frank replied thoughtfully. "We can return it later."

Joe checked his watch. "It's time to hook up with Andrea. Let's finish packing and go."

After stopping briefly to refuel on hot chocolate and apple strudel, Joe and Frank found their way to Andrea Wells's room and knocked on the door.

"Come on in!" Andrea shouted through the door.

Joe saw her seated on the floor amid a disorderly heap of electronic gear and camera equipment with four black-and-white eight by ten prints of the detonator spread out in front of her.

"Hi, guys," Andrea said, scooping up the prints and handing them to Joe. "Here are Frank's photos. I looked through some of the dictionaries in the hotel's reading room and found that's definitely Russian lettering."

Joe looked carefully at each photo before handing them to Frank. "I don't see any clues here besides the detonator itself. At least we can track the serial number, though. Say, Andrea, have you heard any more on Ken's condition?"

"I was just about to call the hospital," Andrea replied, jumping lightly to her feet and going over to the hotel phone.

"Ask if Ivana has been there," Frank said.

Andrea nodded. She started speaking quietly in German as Frank motioned to Joe to come over to the corner of the room.

"What's up?" Joe asked softly.

"A Russian detonator and a Russian sweetheart, that's what's up," Frank replied. "Put that together with Ken's note, and it really doesn't look good for Ivana."

"I agree," Joe said. "Let's see that videotape and watch Ivana's reaction. That could tell us a lot."

Joe turned as Andrea hung up the phone.

"He's still critical," she said seriously. "His right arm and leg are broken, and he's unconscious. The nurse said Ivana hasn't been there. I would've thought she'd be camping out at the hospital."

"Did you get the videotape, Andrea?" Joe asked.

"It's all cued up," Andrea said, reaching over to the Play button on the VCR. "I haven't had a chance to watch it yet myself."

Joe pulled up a chair for Andrea and settled himself on a hassock a few feet in front of the screen. As the announcer's intro to the competition began, Joe hit the mute button on the remote control and fast-forwarded to the start of Ken's run. The judges' booth was clearly shown on the right side of the screen. Several competitors, including Warburton and Morelli, were clustered nearby.

"Looks like we have a clear view of everything," Frank said. "Now let's watch Ivana's reaction."

"Ivana?" Andrea sounded surprised. "You guys are barking up the wrong tree. She *loves* Ken!"

"Shh!" Joe waved at them to be quiet. "Here it comes." Joe's attention never wavered from Ivana's face as the terrible scene unfolded. First she was watching Ken's run, a little smile playing on her lips. Then, as the avalanche thundered down toward the racecourse, she rose to her feet. Her face was a frozen mask as she stared fixedly at the spot where Ken had disappeared. Then, as everyone around her started to panic, the blond woman quietly slipped out the back of the judges' booth.

Joe looked over at Andrea. "You may be wrong about Ivana. Do you have any idea where she went after Ken got buried?"

Andrea frowned. "No. I haven't seen her around anywhere since the race."

"Let's play it again," Frank said. "Keep an eye peeled for anyone who doesn't seem surprised."

Joe rewound the tape. The second time through, he kept his eyes on Warburton. Buck wore a bored expression, flipping through a racing program and ignoring Gibson's run. At the sound of the crashing snow, however, he dropped the magazine and looked up with a shocked expression on his round face.

"Did you see that?" Frank cried. "Play it back and watch Morelli."

Joe quickly rewound the tape. Morelli was just visible in the corner of the screen. He, too, was apparently ignoring Ken Gibson's run, staring fixedly at his electronic wristwatch. But when the avalanche came through the crevasse, Morelli raised his dark eyes from his watch and looked intently in the direction of the avalanche.

"He doesn't look too surprised about the avalanche, does he?" Joe asked.

"No," Frank replied slowly, "but Morelli's already shown us he's a cool customer."

Joe blew out a long sigh. "Yeah, he could have been timing Ken's run." He shook his head. "Well, thanks for getting us the tape, Andrea."

"No problem, guys." Andrea let them out the door. "Let me know if there's anything else I can do. And don't forget, this is my exclusive."

When they were out in the hallway, Joe turned to Frank. "Where do we go from here?"

"Let's look for Ivana," Frank suggested.

"I haven't seen Ivana anywhere," Hans said.

Joe stood at the base of the slope, outside the small booth where Hans operated one of the gondolas. He saw Frank, with his snowboard under his arm, approaching from the direction of the base lodge. "Well, thanks, Hans. Will you let us know if you do see her?"

"Sure, Joe," Hans said. "See you later." Hans ducked back inside the booth and turned his attention to the control panel just as the big gondola came gliding down to the loading platform.

"Anyone see her?" Frank asked.

"Not here. How about at the hotel?"

Frank shook his head.

"Then let's hit the slopes and see who we can find." Joe grabbed his own board, and they jumped aboard the gondola just as it was pulling out.

As the gondola rode slowly up its cable, Joe used Frank's binoculars to scan the mountainside.

"Hey, Frank!" he exclaimed. "There's Warburton, on that chair lift straight across from us, headed up the mountain."

"That lift unloads farther up the slope than this gondola," Frank said. "Let's be ready for him."

Moments later Frank and Joe were racing down the slopes toward one of the huge steel pylons that supported the chair lift. In unison they leaned forward and to the right, angling the right edge of their boards to turn sharply toward the pylon.

They ducked out of sight just as Warburton came flying over the hill above them. As Warburton passed by, both Hardys swiveled their boards so they were facing downhill and started off with quick hops into the air. Frank went first, with Joe in quick pursuit.

Joe saw trees whizzing past so fast they seemed a blur. The speed was exciting and a little scary. He and Frank had trouble keeping up with Warburton, who rode down at breakneck speed.

For the next half hour Joe and Frank followed Warburton onto the ski lifts, being careful to stay well behind him in the lift lines. To Joe's disappointment, Warburton remained totally alone. He spoke to no one and didn't even acknowledge the waves of the fans and fellow snowboarders he encountered on the slopes.

Suddenly Warburton disappeared around a sharp bend in the slope, leaning over far to the left to drag his glove a few inches in the snow and carve a smooth arc as he turned.

Joe tried to copy Warburton's easy grace and managed a reasonable imitation of the turn. But when he and Frank went through the turn, Warburton was no longer ahead of them. It was as though the burly, black-clad shredder had vanished.

"Unbelievable," Joe muttered in bewilderment as he turned into the slope to stop.

Frank stopped beside Joe and looked around. "Where'd he go?"

"Beats me," Joe replied. "Unless he grew wings."

Joe and Frank scanned the slopes ahead of them but could see no sign of Warburton among the skiers and snowboarders.

On a hunch Joe looked behind and saw Warburton bearing down from upslope.

"Yo—Frank, we've got company," Joe said quickly.

Seconds later Warburton shot between them, crouched low over his board. He slid to a sharp stop, facing them.

"You punks have been following me for almost

an hour. I want to know why," Warburton demanded, anger glittering in his dark eyes.

"Hey, man, we were trying to pick up some pointers," Joe said quickly.

"Well, find someone else's moves to copy," Warburton ordered. "I don't want anything to do with any friends of Ken Gibson."

"Hey, show some respect," Joe said angrily. "The man's badly hurt."

"If Gibson's hurt, that's tough," Warburton snarled. "Maybe he deserves it for being so arrogant."

Warburton heeled his board around, then looked over at the Hardys. "Don't let me catch you two wimps following me again, or you could get hurt, you understand?"

Without waiting for a reply, Warburton set off downhill in a burst of speed. Knowing they wouldn't be able to keep up, Joe motioned to Frank to stay put.

"That was a big waste of time," Joe complained.

"Yep," Frank agreed. "I'm ready for a break. You want to head back to the lodge?"

Joe nodded and set off down the slope, with Frank right behind him. As he zoomed around a mogul, Joe suddenly grew aware of a loud grinding, roaring sound coming from the hill above them.

"*Now* what?" he heard Frank holler over the wind.

Joe glanced over his shoulder. His answer

caught in his throat. One of the resort's Sno-Cats was bouncing over the hill at top speed.

It took only a second for Joe to realize that there was no one at the controls—and another second to realize that the Sno-Cat was headed right for them!

Chapter

8

"FRANK—GET OUT OF THE WAY!" Joe shouted
just before he awkwardly pitched himself out of
the Sno-Cat's path.

Frank shot a look over his shoulder at the vehicle. It was so close, it seemed to blot out everything above him.

At the last moment Frank crouched down low
over his snowboard and rocked his upper body
to the right. He tumbled over on his side, and
then the Sno-Cat was right beside him. Frank's
ears were filled with the roaring of the diesel
engine as his face slammed into the hard-packed
snow.

A moment later the sound had passed, and
Frank was looking at the rear of the Sno-Cat.
He saw Joe unsnap his bindings and sprint down-

hill after it, pouring on the speed and making a wild leap onto the Cat's running board.

As Frank reached down to unfasten his own bindings, he heard a sharp grinding of the Sno-Cat's gears. He looked up and saw that it had lurched to a stop.

Frank scrambled to his feet, then ran downhill to join Joe.

Joe had jammed his hand under the steering wheel and pulled out a bundle of ignition wires that had been cut and crudely spliced together.

"The thing was hot-wired," Joe told him.

"That figures," Frank said, leaning in closer to look at the wires.

"I bet Warburton did it," Joe speculated. "We saw him just before the Cat tried to crush us."

"Circumstantial evidence," Frank observed. "But there is a way to get some solid proof. Maybe I can get some fingerprints off the steering wheel and the gearshift knob." Frank began digging through his backpack.

"Don't tell me you have a fingerprint kit in there," Joe said in disbelief.

"Nope." Frank shook his head. "I'm going to improvise one, though."

Frank quickly took out a couple of lead pencils, his pocketknife, and a roll of clear medical tape. He split the pencils open, then shaved the pencil leads into a pile of grayish dust on a piece of notebook paper. Before he could begin dusting for prints, some curious skiers and resort

69

staffers showed up, lured by the sight of the Sno-Cat parked in the middle of the slope.

"I'll keep them out of your hair," Joe volunteered. He wandered over to tell the crowd about the Sno-Cat's getting loose, while Frank climbed into the driver's seat and began carefully blowing dust all over the steering wheel and gearshift knob. Then, when there was a thin layer of gray dust covering those surfaces, Frank picked up any visible fingerprints by pressing the sticky side of the tape down over the prints. He finished by smoothing the tape down on pieces of clean white paper.

"How's it going?" Joe asked as Frank was putting the pieces of paper inside his notebook.

"I'm done," Frank answered.

"What are you going to do with the fingerprints?" Joe inquired.

"Give them to Inspector Kempf to see if they match up with any prints the cops found in Ken's room, or on that detonator," Frank replied as he closed up his backpack.

"Let's go see Kempf right away," Frank suggested as he climbed out of the Sno-Cat.

An hour later Frank found himself sitting beside Joe in Inspector Kempf's stuffy office, explaining to Kempf for the third time his reasons for taking fingerprints off the Sno-Cat.

Kempf's blue eyes narrowed in his round face as he asked, "But why did you interfere with a piece of evidence, Herr Hardy?"

"Like I've been trying to tell you, Inspector," Frank said in exasperation, "I thought it was important to get prints to you immediately. There were a lot of people around, and I was afraid someone would smudge them before you arrived."

"What's the problem?" Joe asked. "Aren't the prints any good?"

Kempf glared at Joe before answering. "They are adequate, but that is not the point. Investigating these accidents is a matter for the police."

"Inspector, we're on the same side," Frank pleaded. "We just want to find out who tried to hurt our friend."

Kempf snorted. "You are out of your depth here. Mind your own business, or you will find yourselves deported in short order."

"But—" Joe began to object, but Frank silenced him with a stern look and a shake of his head.

If we put up with Kempf's lecture, maybe we'll get out of here sooner, Frank reflected. He was just as anxious as Joe to get on with their investigation, but he knew better than to argue with an angry policeman.

It was another half hour before Kempf finally dismissed them.

"Well, I've had more fun at a laundromat," Joe observed. "What do we do now?"

"Let's head back to the lodge and find Hans or some of the resort staff and see what they know about our suspects," Frank suggested.

"We could try the employees' lounge," Joe suggested.

As soon as they arrived back at the resort, Frank and Joe followed the desk clerk's directions to the employees' lounge inside a long, low, one-story structure attached to the hotel's main kitchen.

Stepping through the front door, Frank quickly scanned the rows of wide tables where the hotel and ski resort staff ate.

"There he is, Frank," Joe said, pointing out Hans, who sat at a table in the far corner surrounded by several other teens. Frank recognized one or two of them from the slopes.

"Come on," Frank said, making his way past the tables crowded with people dressed in red and black waiter's uniforms, kitchen whites, or the gray slacks and blue blazers worn by the hotel clerks and bellmen.

"Hello, Hans," Frank said as he and Joe approached the table. Hans looked up from his plate of boiled red cabbage, sauerbraten, and potato dumplings and smiled back.

"Ah, the two American brothers," Hans said. "What's shaking, fellows?"

"We need to talk to you," Joe told him seriously. "Mind if we sit down?"

"I always like a chance to practice my English," Hans told them as two teens sitting on one bench moved over so Frank and Joe could sit down.

"We want to find out more about what happened to Ken Gibson," Frank said in a low voice as he lowered himself to the bench.

"What a drag, huh?" Hans said sympathetically. "Gibson's a nice guy."

"The avalanche that buried Ken was no accident," Joe told him. "Since he's our friend, my brother and I are kind of—looking into it.

"We need information on some people, but we don't want it broadcast around that we're asking questions. Inspector Kempf might not like it, you know?"

Hans looked very interested. "Hey, anything I can do to help, I'll do. And I can keep my mouth shut."

"That's good," Frank said seriously, then cocked his head at the other teens sitting at the table. "But what about them?"

"Don't worry, man," Hans said with a dismissive wave. "They don't speak much English. We can talk in front of them."

"Okay, so what do you know about Buck Warburton?" Joe asked.

"You mean the Ugly American?" Hans replied with a crooked smile. "That's what the local shredders call him, 'cause he's so nasty. I don't know too much about him, but my friend Klaus, who also works here, told me he'd heard Warburton was mixed up with gangsters."

Joe's eyes widened with interest. "Is Klaus here tonight?"

Hans shook his head. "He pulled some ligaments yesterday, so he's at home."

"Exactly what did he tell you about Warburton?" Joe persisted.

Hans thoughtfully chewed a mouthful of sauerbraten before answering. "He said Warburton was working as a strong-arm guy for some Dutch gangsters in Amsterdam. His boss was, um, a loan fish."

"A loan shark," Joe corrected, grinning.

"Right, a loan shark." Hans nodded. "That's all I know. I stay away from Warburton."

"Gangsters, huh? What do you think of that, Frank?" Joe asked.

"It still doesn't prove he's mixed up with the attacks on Ken," Frank said. "What do you know about Ivana Garova, Hans?"

"She's got great form, both on and off the slopes," Hans said with a shy smile. "I think half the guys who work here have a crush on her."

"But what do you know about her and Ken Gibson?" Frank pressed.

"I know they were together for a while. They've had more than one public argument," Hans said. He grinned mischievously. "I guess Ivana's got a bad temper to go with those good looks."

"Interesting," Frank observed, then abruptly changed the subject. "How about Antonio Morelli?"

Hans smiled. "Nice guy. He's a good shredder, one of the best. It's kind of strange, though . . ."

"What's strange?" Frank asked eagerly.

"That he uses such a thick board. Most shredders want flexibility, which you sure don't get with his."

"Maybe he wants greater stability," Frank suggested. "Not everyone who shreds is into acrobatics."

"Maybe and maybe not." Hans shrugged. "You want me to tell you what I know. Another thing," he added. "One of the bellboys told me Morelli always carries the board himself when he's checking in."

Frank nodded. "Well, thanks for the info, Hans. You've been a big help."

"Hey—anytime," Hans responded with a grin.

"It's been a long day," Frank said as he rose. "I think we'll just have some dinner in our room and crash early."

"I'm for that," Joe echoed. "I've been through so much today even my teeth are tired."

The Hardys returned to their room in silence, each lost in his own thoughts. Frank wondered what a thick snowboard could have to do with Ken Gibson's troubles. He tried to concentrate, but his brain was groggy with fatigue.

"We've got a message," Joe said as they entered the room and saw the red light flashing on their phone.

Wearily Frank called down to the front desk for their message. "It's Inspector Kempf," he said after he hung up. "He wants us to call him ASAP."

75

"Swell," Joe said, making a face. "That means we get to spend another couple of hours in that smoky hole Kempf calls an office while we answer his dumb questions."

"You're right," Frank replied. "Let's put him off as long as we can."

The next morning was sunny and cold, and the packed powder made for some fast boarding. Joe and Frank hit the slopes early, determined to stay out until they made progress on the case. They had only been out for fifteen minutes, though, when Frank said, "Uh-oh. We're being followed."

There were only a few other skiers on the slopes, so Frank was certain the solitary black-and-gray-clad skier was shadowing their every move.

"Who is it?" Joe asked.

"A skier in a dark ski suit. I think he's been on our tail for a while."

"What do you want to do about him?" Joe asked eagerly.

"Let's sandbag him. Then we can find out who he is," Frank suggested.

"Got any ideas how?"

Frank thought for a moment, then saw the chair lift that the workmen had been repairing. Some tools and equipment were piled under a tarp, and Frank's sharp eyes spotted a coil of rope. A devilish look flashed in his eyes as he answered. "I've got it. We'll trip him with that rope down there."

Joe grinned at his brother. "Frank, you're a genius."

With Joe keeping an eye behind them for their shadow, Frank shifted his weight to change course toward the pile of equipment. Fortunately, the rope was close enough that he could stretch his arms and grab it as he went past.

Joe caught up to him and asked, "Now what?"

"We shred downhill out of his sight and stretch this rope about ankle-high. When he comes over the hill, we stretch it taut and knock him off his feet."

As soon as the Hardys had passed out of their shadow's sight, they split up, dismounted their boards, and dropped flat to the ground.

A moment later the mystery skier appeared at the top of the hill. As he descended, Frank gave Joe a thumbs-up sign and they pulled the rope taut.

It worked perfectly! The stranger was down before he knew what hit him.

Joe reached him first. Frank saw him pounce on the stranger and kneel over his torso, pinning his arms to his side. As Frank ran over, he saw Joe pull off the man's ski mask. The Hardys were shocked to see it was the Gray Man!

Chapter

9

"WHAT ARE YOU DOING HERE?" Joe demanded, helping the Gray Man to his feet.

"I've been keeping tabs on you," the Gray Man replied, brushing the snow off his gray-and-black nylon ski outfit. "But this time you got me. To be perfectly honest, I'd been counting on your activities to flush out the crooks who tried to kill my operative."

"What!" Frank and Joe shouted in unison.

Frank recovered from his surprise first. "Wait a minute," he said quickly. "Would your operative happen to be Ken Gibson?"

The Gray Man hesitated, then answered. "Yes. Ken is one of my men."

As Joe stared at the very ordinary-looking man before him, the Hardys' previous encounters with the Network and the Gray Man came flooding back into Joe's mind. Hard to believe that this balding, middle-aged man was, in reality, a tough and shrewd secret agent who coordinated the worldwide activities of the Network, a top-secret intelligence agency.

The Gray Man had the eerie ability to blend in perfectly wherever he went, using only a few costume details for disguise. The Hardys hadn't seen him in many months, but Joe wasn't at all surprised to encounter him here in Austria. They never knew where he might turn up.

Joe fixed the older man with a hard stare. "Okay, level with us. What's going on? Our lives have been in danger here."

"This is neither the time nor the place to discuss that," the Gray Man replied sharply. "I'll meet you in your hotel room in half an hour. For now, I have things to do."

As Joe and Frank stared, the Gray Man used his ski poles to push off and zoom down the mountain. "Well, this sure puts everything in a different light," Joe said to Frank.

"Let's get down to the lodge," Frank said impatiently. "I want to see how much information we can squeeze out of that guy this time around."

Half an hour later Joe heard a quiet knock from inside his hotel room. As soon as the door was opened, the Gray Man checked the hall behind him and then closed and locked the door.

"As cautious as ever," Frank commented.

Joe noticed that the Gray Man had a snub-nosed .44 in his hand, which he quickly returned to a holster inside his gray suitcoat. He had changed from his ski clothes into a conservative gray suit and black turtleneck.

"Caution is how I've managed to live to a ripe old age," the Gray Man retorted as he sat on the edge of the bed.

"So what's happening?" Joe said. "Fill us in."

"Very simply, the Network has been tracking a gang of counterfeiters," the Gray Man replied.

With a quick glance at Joe, Frank fished out the twenty-franc note they'd found hidden in Gibson's shaving kit. "Is this a counterfeit bill?" he asked, showing it to the secret agent.

The Gray Man took the note and examined it. "Yes, this is excellent quality, but worthless. Where did you get it?"

"What brought the Network to Graz?" Joe countered stubbornly.

The Gray Man looked at Joe for a long moment before answering. "Are you trying to bargain with me for information?"

"I guess I am," Joe retorted. "We already know that Ken made a dangerous enemy or enemies. If they're after Frank and me now, then we need to know exactly where we stand."

"I'm with Joe," Frank added. "Whoever tried to flatten us with that Sno-Cat wasn't kidding around."

The Gray Man thought for a moment before

he answered. "Very well. Three weeks ago the local police investigated a wrecked car found two kilometers from here. The driver was dead, killed when his car skidded on some ice and went through a guardrail. Inside the trunk the police found a briefcase containing half a million dollars' worth of these counterfeit franc notes."

Joe whistled. "That's a lot of funny money," he commented.

"You're not kidding, brother," Frank echoed. "What happened then? Did you find out who the driver was?"

"No," the Gray Man replied. "We still don't know to this day. His fingerprints are not on file and his ID was forged."

"How about dental records?" Joe suggested.

The Gray Man shook his head. "We tried."

"What do you know about the rest of the gang?" Frank inquired thoughtfully.

"Nothing," the Gray Man admitted. "Our only lead was a room reservation at this resort, made in the name on his fake ID."

"Is that why Ken Gibson was sent here?" Joe asked.

"We felt that with his reputation as a top snowboarder, Ken could operate in this area without arousing the counterfeiters' suspicions," the Gray Man responded. "We hoped he could learn where the counterfeit bills were printed or how they were being moved from country to country."

"Well, he aroused someone's suspicions, or

he wouldn't be unconscious in a hospital," Joe observed.

"We found that counterfeit note in Ken's stuff," Frank offered. "So Ken must have made some contact with the counterfeiters."

"Unfortunately, they seem to have detected him first," the Gray Man said. "He contacted me four days ago to inform me that his Network codebook was missing. That's how he knew his cover has been violated."

"Did you know Buck Warburton has connections with some Dutch gangsters?" Joe jumped in.

The Gray Man nodded. "Yes. He associates with gangsters from several countries and has, on occasion, done jobs for them."

"Like what?" Frank prodded.

"Like breaking the legs of people who were late with their loan repayments. He is not a very nice young man," the Gray Man commented in a dry voice.

"We have another piece of evidence you might be able to use," Frank said, pulling out the photos he had taken of the radio detonator.

But before he could hand them over, Joe reached over and took the photos himself. "Before we give you these, I want another piece of information," Joe said. "Tell us about Ivana Garova's connections with the KGB."

Joe watched the Gray Man's eyes narrow as he sized up the situation. "You two are tough negotiators. But all right. Garova used to be one of the KGB's top operatives.''

"Was? What happened?" Frank asked quickly.

"She defected," the Gray Man replied. "Gibson was the Network agent assigned to help her get out of Russia. Now, the photographs, please."

Joe handed them to the Gray Man and was pleased to note the expression of interest that spread across the Gray Man's face. "Good work, boys," he said simply.

Joe felt a small glow of pride. He knew from past experience that the Gray Man did not pass out compliments freely.

"Do you think this piece of Russian hardware points the case toward Ivana?" Frank asked.

The Gray Man looked at Frank. "This detonator is not enough of a connection. Are you aware of how many tons of arms the Soviet government sells abroad?"

"Sure." Frank nodded, looking disappointed. 'I've read that selling weapons is one of the Russian government's main sources of foreign exchange."

Joe scowled. "I was starting to think that might be a good lead."

The Gray Man tapped his left palm with the eight by ten photos and nodded thoughtfully. "These may still be very useful to us. I'll try to trace the serial number. There's a possibility I can learn who purchased it."

"Wait a minute," Joe said excitedly. "This is all starting to make sense to me. I read a book

83

once about some KGB spies who ran a massive counterfeiting operation during the fifties, trying to flood Europe with funny money. Maybe Garova only pretended to defect so she could set up this counterfeiting gang."

"That is a possibility, Joe," the Gray Man agreed. "Of course, she knew Ken was a Network agent."

"We don't know how much she knew about his current assignment," Joe said.

"We know Ken and Ivana were supposed to be married at one point," Frank offered. "She would have had plenty of opportunities to search his stuff and find the codebook."

For just a second Joe thought the Gray Man looked startled. "You two have certainly done your homework," he said approvingly. "Perhaps you could assist me in one other aspect of this investigation."

"Sure," Joe said eagerly. "Just name it."

"I have already searched Ms. Garova's room and found nothing," the Gray Man informed them. "If she does have the codebook, she must have it on her person. Since she already knows you two as Ken's friends, perhaps you could approach her without arousing her suspicions."

"Sure, but how can we get the codebook off her if we do find it on her?" Frank asked.

"I will leave that up to you," the Gray Man said as he rose and went to the door. "Here's a phone number at which messages can be left for me over the next few days. Good luck, boys."

He jotted the number down on a piece of paper and handed it to Joe. Then he opened the door, checked up and down the hall, and slipped out, quietly closing the door behind him.

"Hans has been keeping an eye out for Ivana. Let's see if he's seen her around," Joe said as he grabbed the phone.

A few minutes later the hotel operator put him through to the gondola operator's booth where Hans worked, and Joe heard Hans's friendly voice coming over the line.

"Hey, I'm glad you called," Hans said. "I saw Ivana a little while ago. I knew you guys would be interested, so I asked her where she was going."

"Don't let anyone know we're interested, Hans," Joe said. "This is kind of confidential."

"No problem, guys," Hans said. "Anyway, she told me she hurt her knee out on the slopes and was headed for the hot tub to soak it."

"Good going," Joe said. "We'll be in touch later." Hanging up the phone, he turned to Frank. "Hans said she's headed for the hot tub. Do you know where that is?"

"Sure do," Frank said, grabbing his jacket and heading for the door.

Joe followed his brother up a flight of circular stairs toward the gym on the top floor of the lodge's recreational center. The room was full of exercise machines and weights. Frank pushed through the big swinging double doors and on to a smaller room off the gym. Joe slowed down to get a look at the equipment. He was startled when he heard his brother cry out in surprise.

Joe burst through the doors and saw Frank pulling Ivana, in her bathing suit, out of the hot tub. She was unconscious.

"She was underwater when I came through the doors," Frank called. "Search the gym!"

Joe looked everywhere, but the gym was deserted. He returned to the hot tub room, where Frank was leaning over Ivana. "How is she?"

"I think she's been hit on the head," Frank answered. "Did you see anyone?"

"No. Whoever it was must have heard us coming," Joe replied. "But look." He pointed at Ivana's clothes, strewn across the floor near the tub. The zippered pockets on her parka were all open, and the pockets on her pants were pulled inside out.

"It looks like we interrupted someone going through her stuff," Joe said. He grabbed her parka off the floor. "Maybe we can find whatever he was looking for."

Joe felt carefully all along the coat's lining. "Hey, Frank, I think I found it," he called out excitedly. Pulling out his pocketknife, Joe ripped open the lining of Ivana's parka.

A small book with a blue plastic cover fell out onto the ground. Joe snatched it up and opened it. The pages were covered with columns of tiny numbers and letters. It was Ken Gibson's missing codebook!

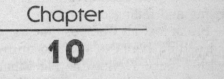

Chapter

10

WHILE JOE FLIPPED through the codebook, Frank focused his attention on Ivana Garova. He had laid her unconscious form on the slatted wooden floor of the hot tub room.

"This isn't good," Frank muttered to himself, wishing he knew how long Ivana's head had been under the steaming water. He paid careful attention to her breathing, worriedly noting that it was slow and shallow.

Frank probed her wrist with his fingers, searching for her pulse. He pressed down hard and found a weak, irregular beat.

Suddenly the unsteady rise and fall of her chest stopped. "Joe, call the resort's first-aid team!" Frank said quickly.

"I'll be back with help as soon as I can,"

Joe called out just before the door slammed shut behind him.

Knowing that his actions in the next few minutes could mean the difference between life and death for Ivana, Frank bent her head back slightly. Next, he opened her mouth and, leaning down to her, began giving her mouth-to-mouth resuscitation. He worked methodically, turning his head after each breath to see if her chest was rising and falling on its own.

Frank lost all track of time as he concentrated on getting Ivana to breathe on her own. It was with a huge feeling of relief that he heard the sound of rapidly approaching footsteps and the door of the hot tub room open.

"They're on their way," Joe said breathlessly.

A moment later three members of the first-aid team dressed in ski clothes burst through the door.

"We'll take over," a tall, dark-haired medic said briskly as he opened his medical bag and withdrew a device that looked to Frank like a small black football attached to an oxygen mask. As Frank stood up, he saw the medic fit the oxygen mask over Ivana's nose and mouth and begin pumping the black ball.

"Hey," one of the medics said in an Austrian accent, squinting at Joe. "Aren't you the kid who dug Ken Gibson out of the snow?"

"That was me," Joe replied.

"You get around," the medic said as he bent

over Ivana and started to examine her. "How did this happen?"

"We just came in and found her over here," Frank answered. "She was underwater, and I think there's a lump on the back of her head."

The tall medic gently felt the back of her head. "You're right. This may not have been an accident."

"We have reasons to believe it wasn't," Frank commented.

The tall man looked for a moment at Frank and Joe, as if sizing them up, then pulled a large walkie-talkie out of a holster on his hip and spoke a few terse sentences in German. Then he listened carefully to the reply.

Turning back to Frank and Joe, he said, "An ambulance is on its way, and so are the police. Inspector Kempf wants you two to stay right here until he arrives. I will wait here, also."

"Oh, great," Frank said quietly to Joe. "There goes our morning."

Frank admired the medics' work as they swiftly got Ivana breathing again and put a cold compress on the lump on her head. A message crackled over the tall medic's walkie-talkie, signaling the ambulance's arrival. Frank watched as the medics lifted Ivana onto a stretcher, carefully strapped her in, then carried her down the winding stairs.

As soon as the stretcher disappeared, Frank heard heavy footsteps and labored breathing coming up the stairs. The doors opened and

Inspector Kempf came through, wearing a dark overcoat. He heaved a heavy sigh. Frank could tell from the irritated expression on his plump face that Kempf was not pleased to see the Hardys, either.

He greeted the medic in German and questioned him for a few minutes, scribbling in a small notebook he had pulled from the pocket of his heavy tweed overcoat.

Frank knew only enough German to understand the inspector's goodbye to the medic. The young man gave a brief wave to the Hardys as he left the gym.

"I thought I made it very clear that you two were to stay out of police business," the inspector said in an aggravated tone after the medic had left.

"We just happened to wander in," Joe replied.

"Somehow I doubt that," the inspector said skeptically. "You two have popped up in too many trouble spots lately. It is against department policy to give out any information on an ongoing investigation, but perhaps I can convince you that this is a serious matter, one that you should stay out of. The fingerprints you took off the Sno-Cat match a fragment of the fingerprints we were able to retrieve from a piece of the light bulb that exploded in Herr Gibson's room."

Frank saw Joe start to open his mouth to ask a question, and he quickly cut him off. "Okay,

Inspector," he said as he glared at Joe to be quiet. "We'll stay out of it."

"I hope so," the inspector said as he slipped his notebook in his pocket and left the gym.

As soon as he was gone, Joe turned to his brother. "What's the big idea?" he demanded. "You're not really thinking about giving up the investigation?"

"No way," Frank replied. "I just didn't want to spend all morning tied up with Kempf. Ivana had the codebook, so we know she's involved. But who tried to take it from her?"

"If we're on the right track, it must have been either Warburton or Morelli," Joe said. "And I think we should concentrate on Warburton."

"Agreed," Frank replied. "I'll search his room, and you try to find out where he was this morning. Do you have the codebook?"

"Yes," Joe replied. "I slipped it into my boot before the medics arrived. We've got to get it to the Gray Man."

"I'll take it," Frank offered. "I'll call that contact number he left us."

Joe pulled the notebook out of his boot and handed it over to Frank. "Okay. I'll head back to our room to get your camera and telephoto lens. After what happened with Warburton yesterday, I don't want to get any closer to him than I have to."

"Good," Frank told him approvingly. "Now you're talking sense."

"Hey, Frank, I just thought of something,"

Joe interrupted. "Did you pack that little parabolic mike of yours?"

"Of course," Frank assured him. "I never know when I might need to do a little discreet eavesdropping. It's in the side pocket of my big camera bag."

"Great," Joe replied excitedly. "Let's get to work."

Frank spotted a Do Not Disturb sign hung on the knob of Warburton's room. First he knocked loudly to assure himself that no one was inside. Then, checking to be sure he was alone in the hall, he set to work picking the lock.

A few minutes later Frank stepped inside. The room looked messy, as if it hadn't been cleaned in days. The bed was unmade, and open suitcases were piled on all the furniture, with clothes spilling out over the floor. Room service trays piled with dirty dishes lay on top of every available flat surface.

Frank set to sifting through Warburton's possessions, eager to find anything that might implicate him in either the counterfeiting scheme or the attempts on Ken's life.

Meanwhile, far up in the hills above the lodge, Joe Hardy crouched behind a snowbank, pointing the parabolic mike's white dish-shaped antenna at Buck Warburton and a tough-looking companion. Warburton held his snowboard under his arm, and the other man was on skis.

Moments before, Joe had taken some photos in which both men's faces showed clearly.

Boy, this surveillance is really paying off, Joe told himself with satisfaction. Warburton's led me right to his contacts. Now, if I can just catch them discussing the counterfeiting operation, we'll have them cornered.

But to Joe's disappointment, Warburton and his squat, bald cohort talked about only one thing. The stranger insisted that Warburton owed him a lot of money and wanted to know when he would be paid.

"What about that job I did for you guys?" Warburton said. "I thought that would square us."

"Not enough!" the short man replied, anger flashing in his dark eyes. "You owe me too much money, Buck. Pay what you owe, or you'll have to do a lot more jobs."

"Hey, Joe, what are you doing?" a cheery voice called from behind him.

Startled, Joe whirled and saw Andrea Wells on skis, at the top of a mogul above him.

Joe frantically tried to wave her off, but it was too late. They'd been spotted by Warburton and his companion.

"Who is that?" the short man shouted, his thick eyebrows shooting up in surprise.

"It's that nosy kid and a reporter!" Warburton yelled.

"They've been spying on us. The kid's got a mike," the stranger growled. "Let's get them!"

To Joe's horror, Warburton began charging up the hill toward them. His companion lagged behind, not able to climb up the hill easily on skis.

"Andrea, get out of here, fast!" Joe told her.

Andrea's face paled with fear, but she looked determined. "Where to?" she asked.

Joe looked around for an escape route. Warburton was closing fast, blocking the slope directly below them. The only other way down was a steep incline to the right of the trail that ran along the edge of a cliff overhanging a valley hundreds of feet deep. It was a risky escape route, Joe realized, but it was the only one left open to them.

"Follow me," Joe said as he strapped his boots into his snowboard bindings and set off down the incline. Andrea Wells trailed right behind him.

"They're getting away!" Joe heard the bald man scream. "You've got your snowboard—go after them!"

Joe sped down the narrow slope as fast as he dared, the deep valley yawning open only inches to his left. He was determined to put as much distance as possible between himself and Andrea and their grim-faced pursuer.

Suddenly Andrea's shrill scream cut the air. Joe turned his head just in time to see Warburton elbow Andrea in the ribs, knocking her off-balance so that she slammed into Joe.

Joe fought to keep his balance, but Andrea's

skis had jammed under his board, and her full weight was thrown on top of him. There was no way to stop or turn as they zoomed toward the cliff's edge.

Joe's ears were filled with Andrea's scream as they both hurtled off into space.

Chapter

11

PANIC FLASHED through Joe's mind as he and Andrea tumbled over the sharp cliff edge. With Andrea's terrified scream ringing in his ears, Joe concentrated on a wide ledge heaped with snow directly below them.

A tense second later Joe and Andrea slammed into the mounds of snow on the ledge with stunning force. Andrea yelled with pain as they hit, and one of her skis flew off into space. Both Joe and Andrea lay flat on their backs, stunned from the impact of their fall and amazed that they were still alive.

"Are you okay?" Joe whispered.

"My ankle!" Andrea gasped through gritted teeth. "I think it's broken."

Joe listened intently for any sound from above

them, and Warburton's voice came floating down. "They went over the edge. Let's get out of here, Otto."

Joe motioned to Andrea to stay quiet. After a few minutes of silence he decided Warburton and his associate must have left. "I'm going to risk calling for help," Joe announced.

For several minutes Joe and Andrea called out at the tops of their lungs, but there was no response.

Despite Andrea's injury, Joe realized that they had been very lucky. The snow had cushioned their impact and saved them. If they had landed another two feet to the side, they would have plunged to their deaths in the abyss. Joe leaned over slightly and peered down into the depths below, trying to judge the distance. It was probably about five hundred yards straight down to a valley filled with jagged boulders.

Joe then turned his attention to the sloping cliff above them. Luckily, the rock face wasn't covered with ice. Joe saw several wide cracks in the rock that would provide just enough of a handhold or foothold to climb back up. Joe calculated the distance and figured he'd have to climb about one hundred yards to get to the top of the cliff they'd fallen from. His flexible snowboarding boots weren't the best footwear for rock climbing, Joe realized, but they'd have to do.

"There's no going down," Joe said to Andrea. "I'll have to climb that cliff."

"What about me?" Andrea asked. "I couldn't climb that cliff even with two good ankles."

"I'll bring back help," Joe said, taking off his parka. "Wrap this around your legs. It'll keep your feet warm."

"Won't you be cold?" Andrea asked with concern.

"I'll be fine. Rock climbing always makes me work up a sweat," he said with a smile. "Wish me luck."

Joe turned all his attention to the rock face before him, plotting the best route to the top. One of the cracks cut diagonally across the rock from the ledge they were on almost to the top. He decided to use that for a foothold and stepped up, wedging his toes into the crack. With his fingers he felt over the rock face above his head and found a jutting piece of rock just big enough to hold on to. Pulling himself up with his arms, he wedged his other foot into the crack. I'm on my way, he thought.

For half an hour Joe made his way slowly up the cliff face, carefully finding a new hold for one hand or one foot at a time. Finally the top of the cliff was within reach, and Joe heaved himself over the top.

"Andrea," he called over the edge, "I'm at the top. I'll be back soon with help."

"I'll be right here," she called back.

Only twenty minutes later Joe was riding the rescue team's Sno-Cat toward the spot where he and Andrea went over. The team set up a sling and attached it to a small winch on the Sno-Cat.

Joe watched as one of the team put a safety line around his ankle and peered down over the side of the cliff.

"Are you okay, miss?" the medic called down to Andrea. "Can you get into the sling by yourself?"

"I think so." Her voice floated up to Joe's ears.

"Use your hands to keep yourself away from the cliff," the medic called down. "We're going to winch you up slowly."

It was only a few more minutes before Joe saw Andrea's relieved face appear over the side of the cliff. The rescue team gently pulled her up onto the ground, and Joe saw that she had brought up his snowboard.

"Andrea, I'm glad you're okay," Joe said, rushing to her side as the rescue team helped her into the Sno-Cat. "Thanks for bringing up my board."

"It was the least I could do," Andrea replied with a grateful smile. Then she leaned over and whispered into his ear, "Now, get back to your investigation. I'll tell the police what happened with Warburton."

When Joe arrived back at his hotel room, Frank and the Gray Man were already there.

"Joe, where've you been?" Frank asked.

"Having the adventure of a lifetime." Joe

sighed as he sank into an armchair. He saw a tray with an insulated pitcher of coffee and a platter of sandwiches, and his tired face lit up. "Hey, is that coffee hot? I sure could use a cup."

Frank handed him a steaming cup of black coffee, and Joe drank it gratefully.

"Tell us what happened," Frank prodded.

Joe reached for a sandwich before answering. "I was spying on Warburton and this goon friend of his when Andrea came up behind me and blew my surveillance. Warburton chased us and knocked us off a cliff."

The Gray Man's eyes widened with interest.

"Luckily, there was a snow-covered ledge jutting out below the cliff, and we landed on that," Joe continued. "Unfortunately, Andrea hurt her ankle."

"How'd you get off the ledge?" Frank asked.

"I climbed up the cliff face," Joe answered. "Boy, am I tired and hungry."

"Are you too tired to hear what I found out about Ms. Garova?" the Gray Man asked.

Despite his fatigue, Joe felt a surge of curiosity as he asked, "What?"

"I checked with my own intelligence people and Interpol, and no one believes Ms. Garova's still with the KGB," the Gray Man said.

"Why not?" Joe inquired.

The Gray Man sighed. Joe knew he hated to give out any more information than he considered absolutely necessary. Joe gave the Gray

Man a hard look, and the secret agent finally answered.

"Because when Garova defected to the U.S.A., she brought with her a lot of very detailed information about KGB spy rings all over Western Europe," he replied. "She can never go back to the Soviet Union."

"If Ivana's no longer with the KGB, then what was she doing with that codebook?" Frank asked.

"And who tried to take it from her?" Joe added.

"If you solve those mysteries, I think you'll know who tried to kill Gibson," the Gray Man answered. "Who are your main suspects now?"

"With Ivana out of the picture, the only logical ones are Warburton and Morelli," Frank offered thoughtfully.

Joe dug into the front pocket of his ski jacket and fished out a roll of film. He tossed it to the Gray Man, saying, "I've got some photos of Warburton and his crony that could break this case. Develop this film and see if you can identify the other guy."

"Did they say anything about counterfeiting?" the Gray Man asked quickly.

"No," Joe admitted. "But I heard Warburton say something about some jobs he'd done for the guy's organization."

"I'll get right at developing these," the Gray Man assured him. "The resort has a darkroom I can use. Then I can fax the photos to our central office for an ID on the second man. Now I must be going. We'll speak again soon.''

Joe opened the door, and the Gray Man slipped out into the hall.

Joe turned to Frank. "What did you find in Warburton's room?''

"Nothing but a big mess,'' Frank replied with a defeated sigh.

"Hans seems to know everything that goes on at this resort,'' Joe suggested. "Let's see if he can account for Warburton's and Morelli's whereabouts at the time Ivana was attacked.''

Joe and Frank went directly to the small lift operator's hut at the base of the resort's main ski slope, where they found Hans on duty. Two of the other teens they'd met at the employee canteen were hanging around, visiting with Hans. Hans introduced them as Erich and Berndt.

"What's shaking, guys?'' Hans asked after introducing his companions.

"Nothing right now, Hans,'' Joe said. "We were just wondering if you or your friends saw either Morelli or Warburton anywhere at about ten o'clock this morning.''

Hans turned to his co-workers and questioned them in German. Joe heard the teens mention both men's names as they answered.

"Berndt says Morelli went up one of the mountain slopes that has been closed all winter, and nobody's seen him come down,'' Hans told them.

"Berndt, what time did he leave?" Frank asked as Hans translated.

Through Hans, Berndt responded that it had been about eight o'clock.

"Erich says he knows just where Buck Warburton was at ten o'clock," Hans informed them. "Erich was on duty at the front desk when the manager called Warburton down to talk about his bill. Erich says he hasn't paid or left a deposit. Apparently, there was quite a scene."

"Where'd he go after that?" Joe asked.

Hans spoke quickly to Erich before answering. "Erich says he got a phone call that was switched down to the front desk. He doesn't understand enough English to know what happened on the phone, but he says Buck was very upset. He left from there, and Erich says he could see him through the window headed straight up the mountain."

"Thanks, guys," Joe said to the group. "You've been a big help."

After promising to join Hans later for a few games of pool at the lodge, Frank and Joe left the hut. "So what do you think?" Joe asked as they wandered back toward the lodge. It was quite cold out, and Joe blew into his gloves to warm his face.

"I think it's time to take a minute to put everything in perspective."

"I agree," Joe replied as they walked toward the lodge. "What Hans and his friends just told us about Warburton's whereabouts puts him in the clear as far as conking Ivana on the head."

"Yeah," Frank said. "So why did Warburton try to kill you and Andrea if he's not involved with this counterfeiting ring?"

Joe and Frank walked in silence for a few minutes. Then Joe snapped his fingers as an idea came to him. "I think I've got it," he said.

"What?" Frank prodded.

"Maybe Warburton's involved with another bunch of gangsters who have nothing to do with the counterfeiters, and Andrea and I just had the bad luck to be in the wrong place at the wrong time."

"Okay," Frank said thoughtfully. Joe could tell his brother was considering all the implications of what he'd just said. "If that's so, then the only reasonable suspect we have left is—"

"Antonio Morelli!" Joe finished his sentence.

"But wait a minute," Frank said. "Didn't Berndt say that Morelli was up on a closed ski slope?"

"Yeah, but if Morelli went up at eight o'clock, he would have had time to get back by ten," Joe pointed out. "Maybe he only went out far enough to drop from sight, then sneaked back to the resort so he could go after Ivana."

"That makes sense." There was an edge of excitement in Frank's voice. "If everybody thought Morelli was out on the slopes, he'd have a perfect alibi in case anybody tried to connect him with Ivana's 'accidental' drowning in the resort's hot tub.''

"Keep talking," Joe told him as they began walking again. "This is all starting to come together."

"Let's see," Frank said. "If it was Morelli, then he must have known Ivana had Ken's codebook."

"But how did Ivana get Ken's codebook?" Joe asked in a puzzled voice.

"Maybe she stole it from Morelli, who stole it from Ken," Frank speculated, adding, "She was an ex-KGB agent. Maybe she used her old spying skills to find out who'd tried to kill her boyfriend, and found the codebook in Morelli's room or somewhere."

"That's pretty good," Joe commented approvingly. "Of course, it's all speculation until we can get Ivana or someone else to confirm it."

Their conversation had carried them to a row of huts styled to look like old-fashioned chalets, which housed the resort's facilities for renting skis, boots, and other equipment. As Joe rounded the corner of one of the huts, he had a clear view of the main lodge's front entrance.

What he saw made Joe stop in his tracks. He elbowed Frank in the ribs and pointed at the entrance to the lodge.

Coming through the lodge's wide plate-glass doors was Inspector Kempf, followed by a pair of uniformed Austrian policemen flanking a handcuffed prisoner. The prisoner was Buck Warburton.

Chapter

12

FRANK AND JOE RAN up to the Austrian police cruiser, a four-wheel-drive vehicle with wire mesh covering the rear windows. Two uniformed police officers put a sullen-faced Buck Warburton into the back of the cruiser with his hands cuffed behind his back. Frank saw him glare at Joe.

Inspector Kempf, who was directing the two policemen, greeted the Hardys with an expression of interest.

"So you bagged Warburton. Congratulations," Frank told him.

"*Danke*," Kempf responded, looking pleased.

His expression turned to one of annoyance as Joe asked, "How did you capture him?"

"That is a police matter," Kempf snapped

automatically, then shrugged. "Well, I suppose it can't hurt to tell you this much. After Fräulein Wells told me about the attack, I alerted the resort staff to watch for Warburton. One of the bellmen saw him sneaking into his room and called me. We caught the ruffian trying to slip out a service entrance near the kitchen."

Thinking quickly, Frank asked, "Was he with anyone?"

Frank saw Kempf's eyes narrow, and he hesitated before answering, "No. Warburton was alone."

"If you can match Warburton's fingerprints to the prints from the light bulb fragments and the Sno-Cat, you'll have him on a charge of attempted murder," Joe suggested eagerly.

Kempf looked at Joe coldly. "You do not have to tell me my job, Herr Hardy."

"I was just trying to help," Joe said.

"You can help by coming down to my office right away and making a statement about the incident with Herr Warburton," Kempf replied.

"He'll be right down," Frank stated, ignoring a glare from Joe.

"As soon as possible," Kempf ordered. "There are many forms to fill out."

Joe rolled his eyes and sighed. "Could I get a ride with you, Inspector?"

Kempf shook his head. "No. Since we have a prisoner in the car, regulations forbid transporting anyone else. You will have to find your own way down the mountain."

With those words Kempf climbed into the front passenger seat of the police cruiser and signaled for the driver to go. Frank could see Warburton slumped in the backseat, staring at the floor.

As they watched Kempf drive off toward the road to Graz, Joe looked at his brother and made a sour face. "Great," he said sarcastically. "That square-headed Austrian cop will keep me cooped up for hours. And you know how much I love filling out forms."

"Put up with it, Joe," Frank said. "We may need all the help Kempf can give us to smash this counterfeiting ring. Besides, while you're down there, at least the best of us will still be out investigating."

"Thanks, Frank. That makes me feel a whole lot better," Joe replied.

Then he turned serious again. "We've got one suspect left—Morelli. I want to go after him."

"It's got to be Morelli," Frank agreed. "He was the only other person here who was around Gibson during one or more of the attempts on his life."

"But why would Morelli be involved with counterfeiters?" Joe wondered. "From what I read in the snowboarding mags, he's just a playboy from a rich family. He seems like too much of a party guy to be involved in something as serious as counterfeiting and attempted murder."

"Hans mentioned that he disappears for long periods of time," Frank said thoughtfully.

"Well, yeah," Joe admitted. "And he wasn't too helpful about the spool episode, even though he was all buddy-buddy with Ken right afterward. In fact, now that I've had more time to think about it, it did seem kind of weird the way he was staring at his watch when Ken got buried under the snow," Joe added.

"Well, while you're dealing with Kempf, I'll dig up anything I can on Morelli," Frank told him. "I think a thorough search of Morelli's room is long overdue."

"I'd better arrange for a taxi down to Graz so I can give Kempf my statement," Joe said. Frank could see the reluctance written on his brother's face.

"Take it easy, Joe," Frank said. "If you get too bored, try reviewing the multiplication tables in your head or something."

"I'll keep that in mind," Joe said with a crooked grin. "See you later." He flashed Frank a brief thumbs-up sign, then turned and headed for the taxi stand.

Proceeding in his usual methodical manner, Frank first went down to the lodge's main desk and asked if Antonio Morelli was still registered there.

"Yes, he is, Herr Hardy," the dapper clerk assured him in excellent English. "Would you like to leave him a message?"

"No, that's okay," Frank replied. "Is he in the lodge now?"

"I have not seen him for over a day," the clerk told him, politely adding, "Will that be all?"

"Yes, thanks," Frank replied as he turned away.

Next, Frank tracked down the chambermaid who normally cleaned the rooms on the floor where Morelli was staying.

The maid, a middle-aged woman, spoke some English, and between Frank's electronic translator and the few words of German he knew, he was able to make himself understood.

The maid said she hadn't seen Morelli around for over a day, and he had left strict orders that his room was not to be disturbed.

"Has Morelli stayed at the lodge before?" Frank asked in halting German after calling up the right words on the translator.

"Ja, ja," the chambermaid told him, smiling broadly as she told Frank what a nice man Morelli was, always so polite and such a good tipper. Frank took her hint and handed the woman twenty marks before asking his next question.

"Does he always stay away for several days?" Frank asked.

She shrugged. "Sometimes more, sometimes less. He comes and goes, at all hours of the day or night."

Frank questioned her for another few minutes but learned nothing else of any substance. He thanked her, and the chambermaid replied with a polite *"Danke,"* then went back to her work, pushing her wheeled cart of cleaning supplies down the hallway.

Frank's last stop was at the ski lift operator's hut, where he hoped to find Hans still on duty.

"What are you doing back here so soon?" Hans asked.

"I need another favor, Hans," Frank told him.

Hans's eyes gleamed with interest. "Tell me what you need. You can count on me."

"Put the word out to all the other shredders who work here to leave a message at my room if anybody sees Morelli. I want to know where he goes and who he's seen with."

"Sure, but why?" Hans asked in surprise.

"Maybe I can tell you when this is all wrapped up," Frank said seriously. "But for now, you'll just have to trust me."

As Frank left the lift operator's hut and walked back toward the lodge, he turned and saw through the window that Hans was already talking on the resort's intercom, which was connected with every ski lift, shop, restaurant, and ski patrol hut in the sprawling resort complex.

Figuring he had done all he could to keep tabs on Morelli's movements for the present, Frank decided to return to his room and call the Gray Man to see what he had learned about Morelli. He glanced at his watch and guessed that Joe was probably just arriving at Inspector Kempf's office.

Frank returned to his hotel room and was surprised to find the Gray Man already inside, hard at work on the Hardys' laptop computer, whose modem was hooked up to the phone.

"Glad to see you had no trouble getting in," Frank said dryly. "What did you find out?"

"A great deal," the Gray Man replied. "The Morelli family's construction company is one of the biggest in Italy. After I did some checking on Morelli Construction I found that the company has lost some of its luster."

"What do you mean?" Frank asked.

"The company was doing well until they built a bridge in northern Italy—one of the longest suspension bridges in Europe," the Gray Man said, speaking briskly. "Unfortunately, the company cut too many corners in the bridge's construction. Possibly the concrete was second-rate or the steel reinforcing bars were inferior. At any rate, the bridge collapsed during a storm last year, and thirty-three people were killed."

"That's terrible," Frank said.

"A government board of inquiry laid the blame squarely on Morelli Construction, and the resulting lawsuits and government fines have driven the company into bankruptcy," the Gray Man finished.

"Then we've got a motive for Morelli working with counterfeiters," Frank said, growing excited.

"Yes, we do," the Gray Man said calmly. "It's clear to me that Morelli's back is to the

112

wall. His family's ownership of their business is hanging by a thread."

"I'm on my way to search his room now," Frank informed the Gray Man.

Frank took the precaution of calling Morelli's room first to make sure it was unoccupied. After the phone rang ten times with no answer, Frank was satisfied that it was safe to go over.

Frank quietly walked down the hall to Morelli's room. He cast a quick glance in either direction to be certain he was alone and then began picking the lock. It took almost a minute before he heard the tumblers click into place and he could push the door open.

Frank was surprised to see Morelli's custom snowboard leaning against one wall. No one had seen Morelli come into the hotel today. Apparently, the Italian was able to slip in and out without being noticed.

Frank was struck again by how different Morelli's snowboard looked from any of the others he'd seen. "I don't see how he can move so fast with such an inflexible board," he muttered to himself.

Frank put the snowboard aside and began looking through Morelli's possessions, trying to leave no traces of his search. He noted that Morelli had a heavy winter parka with a fur-trimmed hood lying on the bed, along with some thick fur-lined gloves, yellow snow goggles, and other outdoor gear. He also saw a pair of snowshoes on the floor beside the bed. Frank was just reaching for Morelli's backpack when his sharp hearing detected a creaking board outside in the hall.

He looked over at the door with an expression of surprise. To Frank's horror, he saw that someone was twisting the doorknob. He heard a key go into the lock and knew it had to be Morelli.

Chapter

13

FRANK'S PULSE POUNDED as he watched the doorknob twist. He noticed a flicker of movement under the door. Quickly scanning the small room for any way out, his eye fell on the bathroom door. Remembering the wide window in his own hotel room's bathroom, Frank slipped over to it and noiselessly closed the door.

Frank hoped he'd have enough time to climb out the window. He gingerly unlatched the window, careful not to make any noise.

Forcing himself to move with caution, Frank stood on the edge of the tub and threw the window wide open. Then he scrambled up on the windowsill and eased through.

Hanging by his fingers from the windowsill, Frank risked a look below. The room was on the second floor, but he saw that a mound of snow had been pushed off a path and piled against the building.

Frank knew he had no time to lose, so he let go, hoping there wasn't anything under the snow. He landed hard and lost his balance, falling backward into the snowbank. Then he rose and silently went through an outer door that led into the hotel.

Joe was having problems of his own at the police station in Graz.

"Look, Inspector, I've waited for over an hour for you to get around to interrogating me. I've also already told you everything I know about the attack on Andrea and me," Joe said in exasperation. "Now, how about giving *me* a little information?"

Kempf's round, mustached face showed no reaction. He puffed on his cigarette as he looked over his notes from his earlier interrogation of Warburton.

He's sure taking his time, Joe thought as he waited for the rotund Austrian policeman to respond. For the hundredth time that night he looked around Kempf's cheerless, gray-walled office and wished he were somewhere else.

"Very well." Kempf's head snapped up, and Joe found himself looking into the man's narrow blue eyes. "You may ask one question," Kempf said slowly in heavily accented English.

"Great," Joe said immediately. "Did you take

Warburton's fingerprints yet? Did they match the prints from the light bulb fragment and the Sno-Cat?''

Heaving a weary sigh, Kempf shuffled through some official-looking forms stacked on his desk. He read over them for what seemed to Joe like a very long time before looking up.

"According to the preliminary analysis of Herr Warburton's fingerprints, they do not match the prints found at the other crime scenes."

Suddenly the fax machine on Kempf's desk bleeped several times, signaling an incoming message. Kempf picked up the receiver and spoke a few words of German. Then he hit a switch on the side of the fax machine, and it began rolling out a long sheet of paper.

Curious to see what it was, Joe stood up and made his way around to the other side of Kempf's desk. Engrossed in looking over the fax that had just come in, Kempf did not immediately notice that Joe was looking over his shoulder.

Joe saw a short message in German that he couldn't read, though he noticed with interest that it bore the logo of Interpol, the international police agency. Joe's sharp eyes also picked Buck Warburton's name out of the message in several places.

Then Joe gasped in surprise. He saw a photo of Warburton and his crony that must have come from the roll of film he had given to the Gray

Man to develop. The Network must have passed the photos to Interpol.

"Ah-hem!" Kempf cleared his throat loudly, giving Joe a sharp look over his shoulder.

But then the old man relented. "Actually, in this particular case, you are *supposed* to see this photo," Kempf told Joe, his expression softening slightly.

He showed Joe the faxed photo of Warburton and the short bald man. "Does the other man look familiar, Herr Hardy?" Kempf asked.

"Absolutely," Joe told Kempf, pointing at Warburton's tough-looking companion. "That's the man who told Warburton to go after us. I'm positive."

"Excellent." Kempf smiled, his blue eyes gleaming. "I shall have Fräulein Wells confirm the ID." Kempf reached for his hat and overcoat, which were piled on a chair next to his desk.

"Before you go, can you tell me what Interpol said about Warburton?" Joe asked, planting himself in Kempf's path.

"It was a request to extradite Warburton to Amsterdam in connection with some assaults he committed there for a loan-sharking gang," Kempf said offhandedly as he buttoned up his overcoat. "Now, I have no more time for questions, Herr Hardy. Please step aside."

"Sure," Joe said agreeably. "Then I guess I'm free to go?"

Kempf nodded. *"Ja*—however, I may need to

speak to you again," Kempf said, holding up a pudgy finger. "So do not leave the resort."

"Don't worry," Joe assured him. "We're not going anywhere." At least until Frank and I solve this case, Joe thought to himself.

Joe hurriedly left the grim two-story police station. He stood on the sidewalk gratefully drawing in big lungfuls of the cold, crisp mountain air.

"Man, it was stuffy in there," Joe said to himself. "Kempf must have smoked twenty cigarettes. Blechh!"

Spotting a taxi idling along the curb fifty feet down the street, Joe trotted over to it and hopped in, and twenty minutes later climbed out in front of the lodge.

As he opened the door of their hotel room, Joe saw Frank putting on his ski jacket and picking up a backpack stuffed with his camera, parabolic mike, translator, and other surveillance gear.

"I know that look, Frank," Joe said eagerly. "Where are we headed?"

"Out to do a little spying," Frank answered. "And there's no time to lose. Grab your board and come on."

"So what did you and the Gray Man find out?" Joe demanded as he followed Frank down the hall to the elevator.

"We learned that Morelli's family business is in deep trouble and figured he might be desperate enough to do anything for cash. I told Hans to alert the other shredders who work here to keep an eye peeled for Morelli. One of them spotted him going up the mountain. He could be headed for a meeting with the counterfeiters."

"Are we going to try and catch him in the act?" Joe asked..

"Yes, but we're just going to get pictures and maybe a tape recording of their conversation through the parabolic mike," Frank said. "The Gray Man insisted we let the cops pick them up."

"Aw, what a bunch of spoilsports," Joe said. The elevator arrived, and he and Frank stepped inside.

"Joe, these guys are dangerous," Frank told him as the doors slid shut. "They've already tried to kill more than once. They play for keeps."

Once downstairs they hurried outside. As they walked over to the gondolas, Joe filled Frank in on what had happened in Kempf's office.

When they arrived at the operator's hut, they found Hans there, sitting by the intercom. "Hi, guys," Hans said, flashing them a tired-looking grin. "I'm in touch with the night ski patrollers. Berndt spotted Morelli heading for the toughest slope on the northeast face of the mountain, the one we call the Killer."

"How much of a head start did Morelli have?" Frank inquired.

"Five, maybe ten minutes," Hans calculated. "You can catch him if you hurry. Ride the main lift all the way to the top of the mountain, then take the trail to your left and go about half a kilometer.''

They followed Hans's directions and found themselves shredding down a steep trail at a reckless speed. The trail soon flattened out, and to Joe's relief, their speed slackened somewhat.

Suddenly Frank signaled for his brother to stop. Joe shifted his weight forward on the deck of his board and leaned his upper body into the turn. This brought his board to a stop in a swirl of powdery snow. Joe quickly dismounted and crawled over to where Frank was crouching behind some snow mounded up against the trunk of a tree.

When Joe· reached him, Frank was already looking through the viewfinder of his camera, to which he'd attached a long, wide telephoto lens. Joe heard the motor drive on Frank's camera whirring as he clicked off a series of pictures. Although the slope was lit up for night skiing, Frank was grateful he'd loaded his camera with high-speed film.

Frank lowered the camera and dug around in his bag for the translator. He handed Joe the parabolic mike, which Joe saw was hooked up to a small cassette deck. Joe trained the white dish antenna on the two men and could clearly hear their conversation through the mike's earphones. To his frustration, the two men spoke in Italian. However, Frank had plugged another

121

set of earphones into the cassette deck and was translating what they said.

"Is it Morelli?" Joe whispered.

"Yes," Frank whispered back. "And he's with someone."

"Can you make out who it is?" Joe hissed.

"No, his back's to me," Frank whispered back. "My binoculars are in the bag."

Joe dug the binoculars out and trained them on Morelli and his companion, thankful for the bright moonlight and lights, both illuminating everything clearly. Morelli's companion turned slightly, and Joe could see that his face was totally covered by a dark ski mask.

Joe saw the masked man say something and hand Morelli a small paper-wrapped package.

Frank translated in a harsh whisper: "The masked guy just said, 'Here's the parcel, Antonio. If you fail us, you're a dead man!'"

Chapter

14

THE HARDYS WATCHED as Morelli concealed the small, square package inside his parka.

"I hope it's worth it. The heat is finally onto us," Morelli said.

"Deliver the package by noon," the other man said grimly.

After exchanging a few more brief words, the two men said goodbye. Then each of them headed for a different trail down the slope, Morelli on his snowboard and the stranger on skis.

"What else did they say, Frank?" Joe whispered urgently.

"Nothing too specific," Frank answered as he began cramming the camera and other gear into his backpack.

"Let's follow him," Joe urged.

Frank gave his brother a skeptical look. "He's taking the slope Hans called the Killer. Do you think we're up to following him down that?"

"We have to, Frank," Joe insisted. "If we let him out of our sight, he could have a chance to stash that package, and we'll never find out what it is."

Wearing an expression of grim resignation, Frank just nodded and pushed off after his brother.

Hans hadn't exaggerated about the Killer, Frank observed. The slope ahead dropped off so steeply that it looked to Frank as if he were flying over the edge of a sheer white cliff. The trees and landscape whizzed past in a blur. Morelli was about three hundred yards ahead on the slope, crouched low over his snowboard and moving at such a high speed that Frank wondered if he could keep him in sight.

Joe and Frank used every reflex to follow at Morelli's speed. The cold air at the high altitude made the conditions dangerously fast—frozen granules that rode like ice beneath the Hardys' snowboards. They both flew down the slope on the brink of losing control.

Before Frank knew it, he saw the lights of the lodge below and felt the slope flattening out. In the distance, Morelli shredded almost to the lodge before braking in a swirl of white powder. He dismounted his board and walked inside, carrying his board under his arm.

Joe and Frank followed Morelli's course, winding up in almost the same spot where Morelli had stopped, though Frank noted that neither of them came to rest as gracefully as Morelli had.

"What's our next move?" Joe asked his brother, panting as they went into the lodge. It was getting late, and the halls seemed pretty deserted. Joe didn't see Morelli anywhere. Anyone still awake was probably at the resort's big disco. Joe could hear the thumping bass of dance music.

"Our best move would probably be to see who Morelli delivers the package to," Frank replied. "If we try to get the package now, we may never find out who the rest of these counterfeiters are."

"Let's get back to the room and get some food and shut-eye," Joe said.

"I heard Morelli's crony say that he had to deliver the package by noon," Frank said.

"If we get up early and stake out Morelli's room, we should be able to follow him," Joe said as they made their way to an elevator.

"That's just what I had in mind," Frank agreed with a smile, then looked thoughtful. "What do you suppose is in the package Morelli has—counterfeit money?"

"If it is, it can't be much. That package wasn't very large," Joe commented.

"True," Frank said. "Maybe Morelli's delivering a sample of the bills."

"We'll find out tomorrow," Joe said with a

125

wide yawn. "In the meantime, let's take it easy. I've had all the excitement I can take for one day."

The next morning the Hardys arose at 4:15 and munched on some granola bars they had in their room.

"I know you wanted to get up early, Frank, but this seems a little too early," a sleepy Joe Hardy said through a mouthful of granola. "I'm not even hungry yet."

"I saw snowshoes in Morelli's room," Frank said, ignoring Joe's complaint. "Wherever he's going, he may need them. Since we don't have any snowshoes, I thought we could stop by the ski patrol hut and borrow two pairs. Hans told me his pal Klaus works there."

"Good thinking." Joe nodded, yawning wide. "You get the snowshoes while I keep an eye on Morelli's room."

Half an hour later Frank returned with the snowshoes and found Joe standing outside the lodge. Beside him, Joe had stacked up their snowboards and the backpack they'd filled with food and other supplies before going to bed.

"Any sign of Morelli?" Frank asked.

Joe pointed off in the direction of a seldom-used section of the resort, whose trails were not well maintained. "He went that way wearing snowshoes, with his shred sled strapped across his back. I made sure he didn't see me watching him."

"Lead on," Frank instructed as he handed his brother a pair of snowshoes.

For hours the Hardys followed in Morelli's tracks, hanging back just far enough so they wouldn't be seen. Morelli didn't suspect he was being followed, Frank guessed, because he pressed on and never looked behind him.

As the morning wore on and Morelli kept up a rugged pace, Frank noticed with some apprehension that the sky overhead was darkening.

"Looks like we might be in for a storm, Joe," he commented uneasily.

Joe looked up, his brow creased in a worried frown. "Yeah, you're right. I hope we don't get caught in a blizzard up here."

As the Hardys neared the summit of a low peak Morelli had passed over, a sudden snowstorm rolled in, slamming them with blasts of freezing snow propelled by gale-force winds.

"We've got to find shelter, Frank!" Joe shouted over the roar of the wind.

Frank nodded, his expression serious. "You're right. If we get caught out in the open in this blizzard, we could freeze to death."

The storm descended on them in its full fury, like a choking, freezing white curtain. Each step was a huge effort for Frank. He was exhausted from fighting the heavy winds and could barely see his hand in front of his face, but he pressed on toward the summit.

As he and Joe fought their way uphill, the snow piled up around their feet, clouded their vision, and clung to their clothes in thick, wet clumps.

Just when Frank felt that he couldn't take another step, the storm relented enough so that he could see a small rock ledge only a dozen yards away that would provide some shelter.

Frank grabbed Joe's arm and pulled him toward the ledge. "Joe—this way!" Frank shouted in his brother's ear.

The storm seemed like an impenetrable white wall as Frank led Joe to the minimal shelter the low rock ledge provided. They made it the last few steps and crouched down out of the freezing, knifelike wind.

"This is bad, Frank!" Joe shouted over the howling wind. "What are we going to do?"

"Stay put until there's a break in the storm," Frank yelled back. "Let's break out the survival gear and dig in."

Despite the high winds, Frank and Joe were able to unroll their vinyl ground cloth and fashion a crude lean-to by weighting down the ends with rocks and both snowboards.

For over an hour Frank and Joe sat within their lean-to, talking quietly and eating chocolate bars.

"I'm sure glad you brought food. I'm famished," Joe said as he shoved the last of a chocolate bar into his mouth.

"It didn't make sense to head up into the Alps without emergency supplies," Frank replied. "We could die up here if we're not careful."

"Cheerful thought," Joe commented, then asked, "How long do you think we'll be stuck here?"

"Your guess is as good as mine," Frank replied. "Look at it this way. It's better than Kempf's office."

Luckily, the storm spent its fury within an hour and moved down toward the resort. Frank heard the wind begin to die away, so he poked his head out from under the vinyl tarp and saw patches of blue sky between the angry gray clouds.

"It looks okay," Frank called over his shoulder.

"Then let's pack up and go after Morelli," Joe said impatiently.

A few minutes later the Hardys were on the move. They strapped their snowshoes on their backs and stepped into their snowboard bindings. Frank scanned the snow-covered mountain slope below them and spotted fresh snowboard tracks in the new-fallen snow.

"He can't be too far ahead of us," Frank said. He noted the direction of Morelli's tracks and consulted his map and compass. Then he looked up from his map with a thoughtful expression on his face.

"Morelli's heading southwest, into Switzerland," Frank told Joe. "There's a mountain village only a couple of kilometers from here. That must be where he's going." Frank looked over the trail ahead, but Morelli wasn't in sight.

"Let's hustle, Joe. I'd hate to lose him when we're this close."

Frank and Joe pressed on through the fresh snowfall. Within half an hour they spotted Morelli snowboarding down a winding switch-back trail below them. It led down to a pictur-esque Swiss village that Frank's map identified as Schwandorf.

Morelli reached Schwandorf while the Hardys were still a quarter mile behind him. Instead of heading right into the village, as Frank expected, Morelli went over to a telephone kiosk and made a call.

"What's our move going to be?" Joe asked as he slid down the snowy hillside after his brother.

"I don't know yet," Frank replied. "Let's see what develops."

The Hardys didn't have long to wait. They had barely concealed themselves behind a row of garbage cans across the road from the tele-phone kiosk when Frank heard the rumble of an approaching truck.

With a grinding of gears a battered green truck rolled into sight and stopped beside the kiosk. Frank saw Morelli step over to the driver's side of the cab and greet the blond, red-faced driver in Italian.

Morelli threw his backpack, snowshoes, and snowboard into the truck's bed, which was filled with hay and surrounded on three sides with high, wooden slats. He climbed into the cab, and

Frank heard the truck being thrown into first gear.

"It's now or never, Joe," Frank said, grabbing his board and running after the truck. Joe grabbed his board and followed his brother.

The truck was old and took its time picking up speed. Frank caught up to it, threw in his snowboard, then hauled himself into the truck bed. Joe poured on the speed, and Frank reached down and took his snowboard, then held out a hand to Joe. With a yank that sent a painful jolt up into his shoulder, Frank pulled his brother up into the truck bed.

Frank whispered, "You check out Morelli's pack. I'll look over his snowboard."

Joe nodded and immediately went over to Morelli's pack and began going through its pockets.

Frank found Morelli's blue-and-white-striped board half buried in the hay and began examining it. On the underside of the board Frank found the shallow outline of a square whose surface was flush with the scratched fiberglass. Morelli had worked snowboard wax into the cracks to try and conceal it, Frank guessed, but he had found it anyway.

He rapped on it with his knuckles, confident the sound would be masked by the roaring and grunting of the old truck's engine. It sounded hollow, and Frank realized it was a secret compartment. Wasting no time, he took out his pocketknife and used its long blade to try to pry up the square of fiberglass.

Frank exerted steady pressure on the square, and suddenly it popped off. Wedged tightly into place underneath was the package Morelli had been given the previous night.

Eagerly Frank tore off the wrapping. The package held a pair of thick, silver-colored slabs. Frank pulled the slabs apart and was shocked to see they were printing plates for a Swiss hundred-franc bill!

Chapter

15

AS JOE SEARCHED through Morelli's backpack, he felt a tug on his sleeve. He looked over, and his jaw dropped when he saw what his brother was holding.

"Where'd those come from?" Joe whispered.

"There's a hidden compartment in Morelli's snowboard," Frank whispered back. "He must have been moving the plates for the counterfeiters to avoid customs searches at the borders."

"Where do you think Morelli and his pal are going with these things?" Joe wondered.

"Probably to their printing plant," Frank said.

The old truck rumbled through the narrow streets of Schwandorf. As he lay in the back, Joe saw that the truck was traveling through a residential neighborhood. The buildings were chalets with wood-shingled roofs, lace curtains, and painted shutters.

Suddenly the neighborhood changed. The buildings were modern with brick and plaster facades. This looks like a business district, Joe thought. The truck slowed and turned into the cargo bay of a weathered redbrick warehouse. The truck lurched to a stop, and Joe heard the clanking of a heavy metal door sliding.

As the door slammed down with a crash, Joe realized they were trapped. He looked over at Frank, who had wrapped the plates back up and was hurriedly stuffing them inside his jacket.

Over the clanking of machinery, Joe heard the truck doors open and slam shut. He grabbed Morelli's snowboard and waited for Morelli to appear at the open end of the truck bed.

As Morelli appeared in the opening, framed by the walls of the truck bed, Joe slid the snowboard toward him as hard as he could. The board shot forward and hit Morelli in the chest. He tumbled backward and hit the ground with a thud.

"Come on!" Joe shouted, diving for the end of the truck bed and grabbing Morelli's snowboard. As he leaped down to the building floor, the driver grabbed Joe by the arm.

Frank slammed the flat of his snowboard into the back of the driver's head, knocking him down.

Joe looked around for a way out. The large room was filled with machinery that he recognized as presses and other printing equipment. There were several men in ink-stained overalls scattered around the printing presses. Two men in expensive suits were sitting at a battered wooden table piled with wrapped bundles of currency.

The air was filled with the clank and hiss of the printing press. Joe spotted a door at the rear of the building and felt a surge of hope. If he and Frank could just reach that doorway, they'd have a chance to get away, Joe thought.

He charged for the door, holding Morelli's board across his chest like a shield. "Follow me!" he shouted over his shoulder to Frank.

As he ran past a bank of lithography presses, Joe shot a sideways glance at it and noticed that a press was running off sheets of uncut twenty-franc notes. Then he saw the two men in suits running at him with outraged expressions on their faces.

The larger of the two, a brutal-looking man with dark, curly hair and a jagged knife scar along one cheek, reached the Hardys first. As he lunged at Joe, Frank plowed into him with his board. The big man went down, banging his head on one of the machines and landing heavily. "Come on!" Frank yelled to Joe as he ran for the door.

The other suited man, a muscular, silver-haired thug, reached into his coat. Thinking he was reaching for a gun, Joe slammed the edge of Morelli's snowboard into the man's stomach, then cracked him on the jaw with the heel of the board.

"I'm coming!" he yelled at Frank as he dodged the falling man, then followed Frank out the rear door of the counterfeiting plant and into an alley.

"Drop the snowboard," Frank ordered, "and help me with this dumpster."

Joe threw down Morelli's snowboard and helped Frank drag the rusty brown dumpster to where it blocked the doorway.

"That should slow them down a little," Joe said with a grin as he stooped to pick up Morelli's board.

The Hardys sprinted to the end of the narrow cobblestone alley. Arms and legs pumping furiously as they ran, Joe and Frank ignored the stares of the Swiss people they passed on the street.

"Where're we going?" Joe gasped.

"We're trying to put as much distance between them and us as we can," Frank shot back breathlessly.

As they ran, Joe hard the sound of helicopter blades chopping the air. They came to a street corner, and Joe noted the street names so he could tell the authorities where the counterfeiting plant was. Below the street signs was another sign bearing the symbol of a helicopter.

Joe stopped in his tracks. "I know how we can escape, Frank!" Joe yelled. "Listen. There's a heliport nearby."

A grin spread across Frank's face. "Maybe we can rent a copter. We could be back at the resort in half an hour."

"Come on!" Joe yelled. Following the rising sound of helicopter engines, Joe trotted as fast as he could. Morelli's snowboard felt as if it weighed a ton, but Joe knew it could be used as evidence and gripped it tightly.

As they reached the intersection of two streets lined with more Swiss chalets, Joe looked left and up a hill. At the top of the hill was the heliport, a small operation with three landing pads, a hangar, and a small operations shack.

There were two helicopters in sight, and the blades on one of them were chopping the air. Joe saw a thin man wearing a leather jacket leaning into its cockpit.

"That guy looks like a pilot, Frank," Joe said with relief. "Let's go talk to him."

The Hardys hurried up to the pilot, a serious-looking young Swiss man.

"Hi," Joe said breathlessly "Er, do you speak English?" he asked.

"*Ja,* I speak English," the pilot said slowly, choosing his words with care.

"Excellent." Frank jumped in. "We're in a jam. Can we hire this copter to take us to the ski resort at Graz?"

"Yes, you can," the pilot said agreeably. "Come to the office, and we can make the arrangements."

"Frank, take care of that," Joe said.

"Okay," Frank agreed. "What are you going to do?"

"Call Mr. Gray and tell him where that printing press is located," Joe said with a grin as he headed for a nearby pay phone.

Frank turned to the pilot and asked, "How long will it take to fill out the papers?"

"Less than five minutes," the pilot assured him.

A few minutes later Frank and the pilot joined Joe near the copter, where he was waiting. "Get in. You can put your boards in the cargo compartment behind the rear seats," the pilot informed them.

With a feeling of vast relief, Joe opened the rear door of the copter's cabin. Frank handed him the snowboards and backpack, and Joe tossed them into the cargo area. Then he climbed in and strapped himself into one of the passenger seats, while Frank climbed into the other.

The pilot was already strapped in and had begun his preflight check. Joe and Frank exchanged nervous glances while they waited for him to finish.

Joe looked down the hill and caught a quick glimpse of someone running along the street parallel to the heliport. "Hey, there goes Morelli!" he shouted.

With a high-pitched whine the helicopter's engine revved. A moment later the helicopter lifted off the pad.

"Ya-hoo!" Joe shouted. "We're out of here."

"Man, what a relief," Frank said gratefully.

"How long do you think it'll take Morelli and his gang to figure out where we went?" Joe asked.

Frank shrugged. "It depends on how much time they waste searching Schwandorf. We may have enough of a lead to get away clean."

Joe couldn't help being a little nervous. Morelli had shown himself to be a ruthless and dangerous enemy, and there was no reason to think that his accomplices were any less dangerous.

Joe forced himself to focus instead on the magnificent view that stretched out below—a line of jagged snowcapped peaks. As they approached the part where they'd been trapped by the sudden storm, Joe said, trying to relax, "Now, this is the way to travel! In a few minutes we can fly over terrain it took us hours to cross on foot."

The helicopter's radio suddenly crackled to life, and Joe heard someone speaking rapidly in German. The pilot turned his head and looked at him with an expression of concern. "We have company, gentlemen."

"What do you mean?" Joe asked in surprise.

"We are being followed by my company's other helicopter," the pilot said seriously. "The pilot informs me that his passengers are armed. They have ordered us to land immediately or be fired upon."

Joe saw the pursuing helicopter pull abreast of them. The side door was pushed open, and

Morelli's Swiss cohort sat on the floor of the copter with his feet dangling out into space. In his big hands was a black Uzi machine gun that looked like an oversize automatic pistol with a folding stock, a stubby barrel, and a long clip of ammo sticking down from its handle.

As the other copter drew even with them, the Swiss crook brought the Uzi up and snapped off a couple of shots into the air.

Their pilot turned to look at the Hardys with an expression of panic. "This is more than I bargained for! I'm going to do what they say!" he shouted, an edge of fear in his voice.

Joe looked beyond the pilot at the plume of snow blowing off the peak over the resort and got an idea.

"Hold on!" Joe ordered. "Fly into that plume of snow and go down low. We're going to jump out."

"Are you nuts?" Frank yelled.

Joe shook his head. "No. I have a plan. If we jump out with our snowboards on, we can be moving as soon as we hit."

Understanding glimmered in Frank's eyes. "That just might work, Joe, and if we hug the tree line on our way down, he won't have a clear shot at us."

The helicopter pilot was white-faced with fear as he put his helicopter into a steep dive. Joe put his boots into his bindings and strapped Morelli's snowboard on his back.

Joe opened the door on his side as the copter

descended into the plume of swiftly blowing snow. He felt a blast of icy wind tearing at him as he hung his legs out the open door. He paused only long enough to fit his goggles over his eyes.

"Geronimo!" Joe shouted. Then he leaped into the whiteness.

Chapter

16

A HEARTBEAT LATER Frank hurled himself out of the helicopter into the swirling white snow. To his relief, he fell only fifteen feet and landed in a deep bank of soft powder.

As he fought his way out of the snowbank, Frank heard the helicopter pull away and felt the cold blast of its propeller wash snow in his face.

Frank pulled himself up on the crust of the snow and spotted Joe almost a dozen yards downslope. Joe saw him and waved an arm overhead to indicate that he was all right.

Frank pulled himself upright and boarded downhill toward his brother. Behind him he heard what sounded like an echo of their copter's rotor blades. In a flash Frank realized the sound was coming closer and knew it was Morelli's copter.

As he pulled abreast of Joe, Frank heard far-off popping sounds and saw puffs of snow exploding all around them.

"They're shooting at us, Frank!" Joe shouted.

"No kidding!" Frank retorted. "Let's shred out of here!"

Frank followed Joe down a steeply sloping traverse that led down into a stand of pine trees. The Hardys zoomed down at top speed, slaloming tightly around tree trunks. Frank ducked under branches, the pine needles whipping into his eyes.

Morelli's helicopter pursued them, coming terrifyingly close to the trees. The red-faced gunman emptied several clips of ammunition into the trees around them. Frank and Joe were moving so fast and zigzagging among the tree trunks so wildly that none of the shots hit them.

Following Joe's lead, Frank kept slaloming in and out of the trees. It was hard work and required his intense concentration as he turned so close to tree trunks that he had to duck under snow-covered branches.

The copter paralleled their downhill course for several more minutes, then peeled off.

"Frank, I think we lost them!" Joe cried out.

"I hope you're right!" Frank shouted back, though he thought to himself that Morelli wasn't the type to give up so easily.

They kept boarding through the woods as they

descended. Suddenly the trees became sparser. Frank glanced around and realized that they had made it onto one of the resort's slopes.

"Keep heading downhill," Frank called to his brother. "This slope ought to feed right into the ski lodge."

"Got you, Frank," Joe replied with a smile.

In less than ten minutes Frank topped a rise and saw the lodge and outbuildings scattered below them. The slope was dotted with skiers. Then he saw something that sent a jolt of adrenaline surging through his veins. He spotted Morelli's copter squatting on the ski lodge helipad.

Frank crouched low over his board and leaned forward to pick up speed so he could pull even with Joe.

"Joe, do you see Morelli's copter down there?"

"Yeah," Joe replied, looking slightly worried. "I know they'll be waiting to ambush us. What are we going to do?"

Frank thought for a moment, then got an inspiration. "We'll ambush them first."

Joe smiled. "How? We don't have any weapons."

"We'll make some," Frank told him.

"Oh, yeah? From what?" Joe demanded.

"From snow." Frank said with a devilish grin. "Let's stop for a minute and make our ammo."

Frank steered toward a deep snowbank and slid to a stop. He and Joe hopped off their boards and began making hard-packed snow-balls. Then Frank emptied the contents of his pack into their tarp. He wrapped the tarp into a tight bundle and buried it in the snowbank, mark-ing the spot with a red bandana.

Noticing the odd look Joe gave him as he bur-ied the bundle, Frank explained, "I need the pack to carry our ammo. We can retrieve this stuff later."

When they'd made twenty snowballs, Frank filled the pack and looked up at Joe with a deter-mined expression. "Let's go get them!"

"Right on!" Joe agreed.

When they hit the slopes, Frank's nerves tin-gled with anticipation for the coming battle.

The Hardys boarded downhill, scanning the slopes ahead for Morelli and his cohort.

Frank spotted them waiting beside an empty lift operator's hut. "There they are," he told Joe, pointing to the hut. Shading his eyes with a hand to get a better look at their enemies, Frank noted, "Looks like they're both armed. Morelli and the other guy have their hands inside their coats."

"Let's split up," Joe suggested. "If we slalom in and out of the other skiers, we can get right on top of them before we're spotted."

Frank tossed Joe six snowballs, then peeled off. He leaned on the nose of his board in a crouch, trying to squeeze every bit of speed out of his board. Frank felt his pulse pound with excitement as he topped the last mogul above the lift operator's hut. He pulled out a snowball for each hand.

Suddenly Morelli's eyes got wide, and Frank realized he'd been spotted. Frank picked the Swiss as his man and bore down on him at breathtaking speed.

As the Swiss man brought his Uzi up, Frank let fly with both snowballs. Instinctively the Swiss ducked. The first snowball missed, but then the second ball of hard-packed snow and ice hit him right in the eye.

Frank steered right toward the Swiss and slammed into him with his full body weight, causing the Swiss to lose his grip on his weapon. With a hoarse groan the Swiss collapsed in a heap. Frank threw himself on top of the man, and as he thrashed around in the snow for his dropped gun, Frank hammered his jaw with a quick one-two combination that put the man out.

Frank looked up to see that Joe had knocked Morelli off his feet and was shoving the Italian's face into the hard-packed ski slope.

"Hold on to him, Joe!" Frank yelled.

Then Frank quickly pulled off the Swiss's belt and used it to tie his hands behind his back before going over to help Joe restrain Morelli.

"That about wraps it up," Frank said, both excited and relieved. "The only things left to do are to turn these prisoners over to Kempf and brief him on what happened."

"No!" Joe protested, slapping a hand to his forehead in his best ham-it-up style. "Anything but Kempf, please, Frank. I'll wash the van for a whole year when we get back home!"

"You solved this case," Frank said with mock sternness, hauling Morelli to his feet. "Now you have to pay the consequences."

The next morning Frank and Joe joined the Gray Man for breakfast at a booth in a remote corner of the large dining room, where he could sit with his back against a wall and get a clear view of the entrance.

"How did it go with Inspector Kempf yesterday?" the Gray Man asked as he sipped his coffee.

"Long and slow," Joe replied, buttering a piece of cherry strudel.

"I'm with him," Frank said, looking up from his plate of bacon and eggs. "Kempf kept us in that stuffy closet he calls an office for almost four hours. I timed it."

"Was he satisfied with the case you built against Morelli?" the Gray Man inquired.

"Yeah," Joe replied. "Supplying the counterfeit plates and Morelli's hollowed-out snowboard gave Kempf all the evidence he needed to pin a counterfeiting rap on the guy."

"And since Morelli's fingerprints matched the ones from the light bulb and the Sno-Cat, Kempf tacked on two charges of attempted murder," Frank added. "Morelli will probably get charged for the spool that came flying down the hill, too."

"Now that we've satisfied your curiosity about that, how about returning the favor?" Joe suggested.

The Gray Man raised his eyebrows. "Maybe."

"Do you know why Ivana had Ken's codebook?" Joe asked eagerly.

"Yes. I visited Ken and Ms. Garova in the hospital yesterday morning. She told me she found the book while searching Morelli's room."

"What?" Joe sputtered. "Why didn't she go to the police?"

"Joe," the Gray Man said gently. "After you've been in the intelligence-gathering business as long as I have, perhaps you'll understand. Ms. Garova is ex-KGB. I imagine that it is very, very hard for her to trust anyone."

"But why was she searching Morelli's room?" Frank wanted to know.

"After Ken got hurt, she began using her training to find out who'd tried to murder her boyfriend," the Gray Man said.

"Hold on a minute. I'm lost," Joe announced. "Why did Morelli have the codebook?"

"Ken told me that he assumed he must have tipped Morelli off earlier in the week when Morelli caught him examining his snowboard. That made Morelli suspicious enough to search Ken's room, where he found the book. Finding that is what made Morelli realize he was being spied on. And that's why he tried to kill Ken Gibson."

"As well as drown Ivana," Joe added.

The Gray Man paused and drank more coffee. "And now that I've answered your question, perhaps there's one more you could answer for me."

"Fair is fair," Joe said agreeably. "Shoot."

"I still don't understand how Morelli caused the avalanche that buried Ken Gibson."

"I can explain that," Frank offered. "If you have a Network technician take apart Morelli's electronic wristwatch, my bet is you'll find a powerful miniature radio transmitter built into it. I suspect Morelli used the transmitter to set off a string of small seismic charges via a radio-controlled detonator."

"Frank's theory is probably right," Joe said. "You can see him triggering the charges in the videotape of the competition. Morelli's punching a button on his watch right before Ken gets buried."

"That fits," the Gray Man said quietly. "It was certainly Morelli who set up the detonator and the bombs. The Network was able to track that particular detonator through its serial number. It was part of a load of Russian explosives purchased by Morelli Construction for blasting purposes."

"Well, if that answers all your questions, do you mind if we go now?" Joe asked.

"No, I suppose not," the Gray Man replied. "I'm satisfied. But why the big hurry?"

Joe looked slightly embarrassed. "Well . . . I promised Andrea I'd meet her soon so we could watch the competition today. The slopes have been regroomed, and everything is ready to roll."

"But wait, I'm not satisfied," Frank said to the Gray Man. "We told you and Kempf about the counterfeiting plant we found, but what about the rest of Morelli's gang?"

The Gray Man raised a hand. "Not to worry, Frank. Network agents raided the plant shortly after Joe called me yesterday. They seized all their equipment and bagged the entire gang."

"Why didn't you tell us?" Joe said indignantly.

"No need for you to know," the Gray Man replied as he stood up. "Thanks for the breakfast," he called over his shoulder as he hurried away, quickly blending in with the crowd.

At that moment Frank noticed Andrea Wells entering the restaurant on crutches. She wore a cast on her broken ankle and was dressed in a stylish black and white snowsuit and a black turtleneck.

"Here comes your date, Joe," Frank said.

"Great," Joe replied, but Frank noticed his brother didn't look terribly happy to see her.

"What's wrong, Joe?" Frank asked. "Aren't you glad to see Andrea?"

"Sure, Frank. I was just thinking about the Gray Man. The next time we see him, let's get him to pay us back for the breakfast bill after all we've done for him."

"Maybe he could give us some hazardous duty pay, too," Frank quipped.

Frank and Joe's next case:

Frank and Joe join Andrew Driscoll, the son of a professor, on a critical cross-country train ride. They are acting as decoys in a top-secret plan to transport a deadly virus from San Francisco to Chicago. In the wrong hands, the virus could unleash a biological catastrophe of unimaginable proportions!

But the plan goes haywire when Andrew disappears and the shocking truth about the Hardys' mission becomes clear. The boys begin to suspect that they are the ones ticketed for disaster, and that the end of the line for both them and the virus—is dangerously near . . . in *Terror on Track,* Case #57 in The Hardy Boys Casefiles™.